"There are a lot of things I should be doing, but first..."

Mitch pulled Kate into his arms and kissed her.

She started to object, but he took advantage of her parted lips and stroked his tongue into her mouth, slow and deep, until she helplessly responded.

He had come to her. There had been no games, no lame attempts at seduction. She tasted his need in his kiss, felt his determination in the strong steady beat of his heart against her breast.

She touched his tongue with hers, heady from the warm smell of his skin, from the heat of his body where it pressed intimately against hers. He used his free hand to brush a wayward lock of hair away from her face, and then stroked her cheek with the pad of his thumb.

"You feel so damn good." He kissed her again, hard, his stubbled jaw rasping against her overly sensitized skin.

She knew he wanted her something fierce. But was it enough to ignore his duty?

Blaze

Dear Reader,

For those of you who read *Texas Heat*, you may be wondering about what happened to Kate Manning. Sure, she was engaged, although beset with misgivings, and then Mitch Colter stepped out of the past and into her life, sending her into a tailspin. As a smitten schoolgirl she'd had a mad crush on him, her brothers' friend—older, confident and elusive. Yet he'd still been a boy when he left their small Texas community. Now he's a man, and infinitely more tempting.

I must confess I sometimes wonder about boys from my past. Who are they now? What do they do? Would their smiles still make me giddy? Okay, maybe not. I think I'll let the answers remain a mystery. Or at least let my imagination fill in the blanks.

Happy reading!

Debbi Rawlins

Debbi Rawlins

TEXAS BLAZE

TORONTO NEW YORK LONDON
AMSTERDAM PARIS SYDNEY HAMBURG
STOCKHOLM ATHENS TOKYO MILAN MADRID
PRAGUE WARSAW BUDAPEST AUCKLAND

ISBN-13: 978-0-373-36552-4

TEXAS BLAZE

Copyright © 2009 by Debbi Quattrone

ABOUT THE AUTHOR

Debbi Rawlins lives in central Utah, out in the country, surrounded by woods and deer and wild turkeys. It's quite a change for a city girl, who didn't even know where the state of Utah was until four years ago. Of course, unfamiliarity never stopped her. Between her junior and senior years of college she spontaneously left home in Hawaii, and bummed around Europe for five weeks by herself. And much to her parents' delight, returned home with only a quarter in her wallet.

Books by Debbi Rawlins

1

KATE MANNING JUMPED at the loud pop. She tilted her head back, her gaze going to the explosion of red, blue and silver that burst against the night sky, and then rained down in glittering streamers to the delight of the spectators. The annual July Fourth celebration and fireworks display hosted by her family was almost over. Friends and neighbors would soon leave the Manning ranch, exhausted from the three days of festivities. She couldn't wait for them to go.

She should have been happier. Ecstatic, really. Standing apart from the crowd, she leaned against the kitchen door and stared down at the sparkling one-carat diamond ring on her finger. She was engaged to be married in six months for goodness' sakes. She'd long ago chosen a dress and started making plans for a late-winter wedding when West Texas wasn't so horribly hot.

Her college friends were here, having traveled thousands of miles to join her in celebrating her engagement. Only two weeks ago she'd called each of them herself, and practically begged them to come. A day later the blues had taken hold, and she'd nearly called them back to rescind the invitation. But she hadn't, and now she wondered if subconsciously she wished they'd come to talk her out of getting married.

Another explosion of red and blue lit up the sky, and she peered into the crowd, focusing in the direction where she'd last seen Dennis talking to Clyde Thompson, owner of the Red Rock Ranch. One thing about her fiancé, she thought wryly, he had quite a knack for zeroing in on the wealthy and powerful.

Damn him for missing most of the weekend. He knew how important it was to her that he meet her friends, but he'd skipped the barbecue and dance yesterday, then the rodeo and picnic this afternoon, finally showing up an hour ago. Since then he'd spent his time working the crowd like a seasoned politician. Was that her appeal, she thought uneasily, her family name and community standing?

It was nerves making her short-tempered with him. That's all. Over a hundred and fifty people had shown up this weekend, requiring an enormous amount of preparation to make sure there was enough food and drink. After the cleanup was through, and she'd had a couple nights of good sleep, she'd be back to normal. Happy again that she was marrying such a good man. One she would always be able to count on. One who understood her and loved her. She could continue planning her wedding without all the distractions, which would surely lift her spirits.

Feeling a bit queasy, she wrapped her arms around her middle. One minute, then she'd go find Dennis. So far he'd met Jessica, but not her other two friends. They were both off somewhere with her brothers. Man, she hadn't seen *that* coming.

A breathtaking array of blue and gold blossomed in the sky, quickly followed by a rapid succession of fiery rockets in brilliant colors, which meant the show was building to the finale. Kate smiled at the appreciative murmurs of the crowd, content that the weekend had been a success. Near where the children's rides were set up, silvery white sparklers bobbed in the dark, and she briefly considered turning on the driveway floodlights for anyone wishing to get a head start on the exiting crowd. Or was it a tad too soon?

She turned toward the lineup of trucks and cars, and thought she saw the silhouette of a man coming down the drive. Odd that someone would be arriving only now. Squinting, she waited for the next burst of light. Her breath caught. The man almost looked like…

No, it couldn't be Mitch Colter. This man's shoulders were broad like Mitch's, and he was tall and narrow-hipped, his hair long and dark. He even walked with that slight swagger. But Mitch wasn't even in the country, as far as she knew. God, he hadn't been back to West Texas, much less Appleton, in eight years.

Two months.

And one week.

As the man got closer, her insides started to flutter, and she straightened. No way on earth could that be Mitch.

HE SAW HER STANDING outside the kitchen door. Mitch almost hadn't realized it was Kate. All grown-up, taller than he remembered, and a lot curvier. But the rich auburn hair gave her away. He'd never seen that color on any other woman. She'd cut it, though, to just above her shoulders. Too bad. He'd always liked it long and kind of wild.

As he closed in on the house, he knew she'd spotted him and he reversed his decision to head into the crowd. Instead, he strode toward her and noticed how she suddenly straightened, her stance almost defensive. That he didn't understand. Maybe she didn't recognize him. No one knew he was coming. He hadn't known himself until two days ago.

The fireworks were almost over. He'd been to enough of the Manning's July Fourth shindigs over the years to know that the big finish was coming any minute. Which made him wonder why Kate was standing off by herself.

She moved away from the door and down to the bottom step. "Mitch." She frowned slightly. "Does anyone know you're back in town?"

"It was a last-minute decision." He opened his arms to her. "Don't I get a hug?"

Her lips parted, uncertainty flickering in her face, and then she smiled and moved toward him. "It's good to see you," she said, hesitating a moment before clumsily embracing him.

He slid his arms around her and lifted her off the ground, swinging her in a half circle. It was a mistake. He knew it the moment their bodies touched.

Little Katie had breasts now. Nice, firm round breasts that felt too damn good pressed against his chest. When the hell had that happened?

He quickly put her down. Too quickly, judging by her confused look. And then he really screwed things up by running his hands down her back until his palms molded to the top of her backside. Careful not to make another sudden move, he drew his hands to either side of her slender waist, set her back to look impassively at her, and then gave her a brotherly smile.

"You look terrific," he said, casually lowering his arms.

"I swear you're taller than when I last saw you."

She blinked, and hunched her shoulders. "I had a surprise growth spurt."

Rather than hide her breasts, the action drew his attention because the blue shirt gaped slightly. He abruptly lifted his gaze. Got a grip. This was Katie, Joe and Clint's baby sister. "What's it been, Katie, six years?"

"Eight," she said with faint irritation. "And no one calls me Katie anymore."

"Ah." His smile broadened at the defiant lift of her chin, an old habit he'd found amusing because she'd always been on the shy side.

"What?"

"I promise I'll try to remember."

She drew in her lower lip, studying him for a second, before her gaze drifted toward the crowd. "Your parents aren't here, are they?"

"Still in Little Rock with my sister and her kids."

She sighed. "I'm so sorry about what happened to their cattle. Tom Jenkins and the Reynolds were hit by rustlers, too. The Double R is still in business but they're hurting."

He nodded. Hard to hear even though he already knew the facts. The ranchers in the area had been here for generations so he knew every one of them.

Her lips twisted in a wry smile. "So why are you here?"

"To handle some ranch business for the folks," he said, the grim reminder of the reason for his return taking some of the pleasure out of seeing Kate.

Ranch. What a joke. Only an empty house remained,

and land that had been in the Colter family for over a hundred years. The small herd of cattle that had once sustained the place was gone. And it seemed as if the authorities didn't give a damn.

"I miss your parents," she said, "even though I only spend summers and holidays here anymore."

"You're teaching, right?"

She nodded. "In Vernal. I keep an apartment there because a round-trip takes two and half hours out of my day."

"High school?"

"Heavens no. Middle school is hard enough."

"I bet." He willed himself not to look at her breasts. Bad enough his chest was still imprinted with the memory of them. Her eyes looked greener, brighter, or maybe it was the light coming from the kitchen. "How many of your students have crushes on you?"

"Oh, please." Her cheeks turned pink, and making a sound of exasperation, she tucked a lock of hair behind her ear.

Something sparkled on her hand. Startled, he stared at the diamond on her finger. "I see that congratulations are in order."

"What?" She blinked, and then gave the ring a cursory glance before hiding her hand behind her back. "Oh, right."

"When's the wedding?"

She hesitated. "The end of January. Look, I don't know where Clint is. Joe's upstairs but I think he's kind of busy." She looked up at the sky and then toward the crowd. "I really should get out there and say goodbye to people."

"Of course." He waved her on. "I didn't mean to hold you up."

"No, I'm glad to see you. Really." She moistened her lips and took a step back. "I'm looking forward to talking to you some more," she said as she kept backing away. "If I see Clint, I'll tell him you're here."

Mitch watched her hurry toward the tent and stage area. Kate was getting married? Now why was he so surprised? She was six years younger than him, which made her about twenty-seven. As a kid she'd been on the gangly side, showing more interest in trying to keep up with her brothers than in fashion or makeup. But she'd grown up to be quite a looker, always had been bright and dependable, too. She'd make a great ranch wife.

Nope, there was no trace of the tomboy now, he thought as he watched the gentle sway of her hips. He'd started getting too engrossed in her shapely rear end and had to sternly remind himself that this was Kate. Besides the fact she was an engaged woman, he didn't need Joe or Clint kicking his ass.

KATE HURRIED IN DESPERATION toward the refreshment booth where she thought she saw Dennis. People looked at her as if they feared she were on her way to a fire. Ironically, it was the other way around. The searing heat of flesh and muscle that had threatened to engulf her in a mindless burst of flames was what had her racing through the crowd.

Mitch, here in the flesh. She still couldn't believe it. He'd touched her. Held her against his strong broad chest until she thought she'd suffocate from lack of oxygen. The physical exchange had lasted a heartbeat, but it might as well have been a lifetime. A hundred-odd sensations crashed in on her for which she hadn't been prepared. Sure, she'd had a childish crush on him until he'd left for college, but that was eons ago.

After dropping out of Texas A&M his senior year, he'd started drifting from one job to another and rarely came home. Once she had gone East to school, their paths crossed less frequently. She still thought about him from time to time, but normally only when she saw his parents or the Colter name came up in conversation.

But he was different somehow. Her crush had been on a boy. Mitch was a man now. A damn good-looking man, who by merely showing up, had just thrown her a curveball she could never have anticipated. Had that cleft in his chin always been that deep? Or his voice so low and sexy? Her legs felt a bit wobbly, and it occurred to her that if she didn't sit down soon, she might end up making a fool of herself.

"*Chica,* are you all right?" Maria's concerned voice came from behind.

Kate spun around and saw the older woman with one of her young grandchildren tightly clasping her hand. "Yes, I was just looking for Dennis." Kate smiled at the child. "Hello, Hilda, are you having fun?"

The little girl nodded, her mouth curving in a toothless grin. Maria continued to stare speculatively at Kate. After being the Manning's housekeeper for over twenty-five years, not much got by her. When Kate's parents had been killed in a car accident, Maria had been there to cradle her as she sobbed uncontrollably for hours.

"Have you seen him?" Kate asked, her pulse finally starting to slow down. "Dennis?"

Shrugging her plump shoulders, Maria shook her head. She didn't like Dennis, Kate knew. Neither did her brothers, even though no one had said a word to her. Maybe that was the reason for her earlier funk. He'd not only disappointed her this weekend by showing up late, but he'd disappointed them, and that didn't help. She'd tried to tell them that Dennis was a nice man with a good sense of humor, and all the other things that made her care for him, but in her heart she knew her family thought of her as a kid, and that no man would ever please them.

"Go on," Kate said, making a shooing gesture with her hand. "I'm fine. Enjoy the fireworks. They're almost over."

Anxious to be away from Maria's knowing eyes, Kate quickly wove her way into the crowd, trying to remember the color of his shirt. Brown, maybe? That wouldn't help much. Half the men here were wearing dark colors. Dennis wasn't nearly as tall as Mitch, or so muscular that he could easily lift her in the air. Nor did he have thick sable hair and slate-gray eyes that seemed to darken along with his mood. And there was no comparing Mitch's strong square jaw to...

Briefly closing her eyes, she gritted her teeth. She had to stop this. Not only was her sudden preoccupation unfair to Dennis, but she was only making herself crazy. God, how she wanted a margarita, or a beer. Anything with alcohol would do. Tequila. One shot would calm her nerves. Hell, one shot would probably put her to sleep. She occasionally drank a glass of wine, and she loved a slushy margarita with Mexican food, but that was pretty much it.

She didn't care. Her nerves were buzzing like angry

bees, and she needed the respite of blessed numbness. Heading straight for the refreshment booth, she avoided eye contact as much as possible, but smiled politely when necessary. She slipped behind the bar and found the tequila. After pouring some in a paper cup, she noticed Sylvia Crabtree eyeing her with interest. The woman had a heart of gold but was also capable of spreading gossip faster than the Internet. Kate resisted the urge to slam back the shot of tequila, smiled at the woman instead, then walked away without the drink. Silly, because why should she care what anyone thought? But she did, and that fact wasn't going to change just because she recognized the foolishness of it.

She kept a watchful eye out for Dennis. Most people were focused on the color displays in the sky, while still sitting on the blankets they had spread out for their picnic suppers. She'd already checked out the groups of cowhands standing near the tent with beers in their hands. Anyway, she doubted Dennis would be wasting his time talking with the help.

Oh, brother, she really had to knock off the uncharitable thoughts. Yes, she was angry enough to scream, but she suspected guilt over her reaction to Mitch had more to do with her readiness to pick Dennis apart.

The area behind the bunkhouse seemed to be deserted, the perfect place where she could be alone with her thoughts, pull herself together before saying her goodbyes to everyone. The fireworks would be over in two minutes and the crowd would thin quickly. She'd find Dennis then.

She leaned back against the bunkhouse wall of rust-stained cedar, and closed her eyes, intent on savoring the moment. At the same time, a man's voice came from around the side of the bunkhouse that faced away from the crowd.

Dennis's voice.

Her eyes flew open. She listened, waiting. Trying to convince herself she'd been mistaken. A second later, coming from the same direction, a woman laughed softly.

Kate pushed away from the wall and stood perfectly still. Surely she'd only imagined Dennis's voice. What would he be doing there at the side of the bunkhouse? It didn't make sense. Again, hushed voices and laughter drifted toward her. She struggled for her next breath. Perhaps her body had acknowledged what her mind refused to accept.

Slowly she forced herself to take a step toward the sound. She moved quietly, dreading what she might find. Right as she got to the corner of the bunkhouse, before she rounded the corner, she took a deep breath, fortifying herself. Then she ducked around the corner. The darkness and the ancient oak tree both obscured her view. By the same token, she wasn't visible, either, and she waited another second, listening and hoping she'd imagined the whole thing.

"I have to get back." It was Dennis's voice. "I think the fireworks are almost over."

"Hmm, not yet," the woman whispered seductively.

"Damn, you're making this hard."

The woman laughed. "That's the point."

Kate's heart twisted in a queasy knot. It was obvious what was going on behind the tree. She told herself she should just leave. Why humiliate herself by letting them know she was here? But she couldn't move. She could barely breathe.

Damn him. This was her house, her property, her party. Why make it easy for him by not letting him see her? She loosened her fists, unaware that she had clenched them, and lifting her chin, stepped out into the open.

The woman's back was to Kate. A blur of blond hair and curves, and an indecently short denim skirt. Dennis was pressed against her, kissing her, running his hands down her back. Even though a shadow muted his face, Kate knew the second he noticed her.

He straightened and then jerked away from the woman. "Jesus."

"Bastard." Kate's voice came out a whisper. She couldn't deny she wanted to slap him. Instead, she backed away.

"Wait." Dennis rushed toward her. "Kate, please, this isn't what it looks like."

Every ounce of her wanted to run, hide until the scene faded from her memory, but she stopped, a hint of hysteria bubbling inside her. Calmly, she said, "Then what is it?"

His face was clear to her now, the pallor of his skin, the fear in his eyes largely satisfying. He stared mutely at her. Then he lifted a hand to touch her, and she jumped back, unable to trust herself to remain genteel.

"Leave, Dennis. Now."

"We need to talk."

Without another word, she turned and headed back toward the house, praying her legs would carry her the entire way.

2

MITCH MOVED FARTHER BACK into the cover of the shadows, clenching his fists in helpless rage. Hidden, he waited until Kate had passed by, the man who was obviously her fiancé right behind her, before Mitch dared to relax his hands. The blonde who'd been with the scumbag wandered off in the opposite direction. Mitch had no quarrel with her. Who knew what the two-timing bastard had told her?

Not that Mitch had the right to stick his nose into Kate's business. She'd be mortified to learn that anyone had witnessed her fiancé's betrayal. Still, he wasn't reacting any differently than Clint or Joe would have. Either one of her brothers would have laid the guy flat already. That Mitch had shown any kind of restraint was a small miracle, a testament to how far he'd come from the hotheaded kid who'd left West Texas all those years ago.

The fireworks were over, the last of the red, white and blue from the finale already fading from the dark sky. Dozens of people had started trudging toward the lineup of cars and trucks that stretched for a quarter mile down the private road leading to the highway. He tried in vain to keep track of Kate's movements, but he lost her in the crowd. Although he figured she had to be headed for the safety of the house. Poor kid. He hoped she wasn't stopped by too many people.

Shoving his hands into the pockets of his jeans, he strode in the same direction, staying clear of the lighted areas, not anxious for anyone to recognize him and start shooting the bull. He wouldn't mind running into Clint or Joe, although he knew enough to keep his mouth shut about what he'd just seen. Whatever happened with the engagement, whether she was foolish enough to give the guy a second chance or send him packing, it was up to Kate to deliver the news to her family.

Man, he hoped she did the smart thing. Nah, he didn't have to worry. Kate had more pride and gumption than to take back the bastard. She'd cut him loose. Unfortunately, that was the easy part. The next few days of second-guessing and painful self-doubt was the stage he didn't envy her. The pointless replaying of conversations that had left her uneasy, of the excuses he'd given that she so readily and irrationally accepted. Mitch knew the drill. He'd been there himself once.

Mitch rubbed the tension building at the back of his neck. Damn, he wished he hadn't headed to the bunkhouse. He needed to focus on the rustling problem, and now all he could think about was rearranging that jerk's face.

AFTER BEING STOPPED TWICE, Kate raced though the kitchen door and upstairs to her bedroom. More people would undoubtedly be looking for her to give their thanks and bid her good-night. She didn't care. Better they couldn't find her than breaking down in front of them.

If no one mentioned her engagement, she'd probably be okay, but she hadn't been willing to take the chance. Word would spread soon enough that the wedding was off. Not even if Dennis got down on his knees and begged forgiveness, or took out a full-page ad in the *Houston Chronicle* announcing to the world what a jerk he'd been and pleading for a second chance would she give in.

She locked her bedroom door, leaned back against it and slowly sank to the floor. How could Dennis have been so callous? It was horrible enough that he'd betrayed her, but in her own backyard? The throbbing at her temples intensified until the pain blurred her vision. She squeezed her eyes shut, refusing to cry, the searing sting of tears burning the backs of her lids.

The hazy image of the woman he'd been kissing edged into Kate's mind. She hadn't gotten a very good look at the blonde and couldn't say if she knew her or not. Everything had happened so fast. But she recalled the short skirt and the bleached, teased hair. The kind of woman the cowhands picked up in the local bar for a night.

Kate shuddered. Ironically, one of the problems she'd had with Dennis was that he was a bit of a stuffed shirt. Conservative and proper to a fault, even for a school principal. His goal was to become superintendent of schools for the West Texas district. She understood he needed to protect his image, but how often had she tried to get him to loosen up when they were alone? Yet he'd risked everything by compromising himself at the side of the damn bunkhouse.

Drawing her legs up, she hugged her knees to her chest, hoping to ease the pressure there. She felt hollow and empty and so terribly stupid. How could she not know this man? She'd been dating Dennis for nearly two years. Even when they had no time to share dinner or go to a movie or a play, she saw him every day at school.

"Oh, God." She covered her mouth with her hand, afraid she was going to be sick.

How would she be able to face him? It was one thing to have to announce that their engagement was off, but how could she expect to do her job? Go to her classroom and teach knowing his office was right down the hall, ignore the other teachers gossiping in the lunchroom and giving her pitying looks. She had a month and a half before the school year started, she reminded herself calmly. It did no good.

What a bastard. How many times had he told her how perfect she was for him? How good they were together? What he'd really meant was that she could help his career, she realized with a fresh stab of pain.

Her parents had left Kate and her two brothers a vast and profitable ranch. In the thirteen years since their deaths, under her older brother Joe's leadership, the Sugarloaf had become the second-largest ranch in the county. Although none of them had been politically active, the Manning name meant something in the community. Enough to help Dennis become superintendent of the district.

Anger squeezed out the hurt, and she slowly pushed herself up. Good thing she'd dragged her feet over ordering the invitations and meeting with the caterers. Her excuse had been that she needed to prepare for the July Fourth weekend, but the truth was, she'd effortlessly organized the festivities for the past ten years. Had instinct regarding Dennis's motives made her cautious?

She couldn't deny the doubt that had plagued her lately, which she'd attributed to prenuptial jitters and fatigue.

The phone rang, startling her. It was him. She knew it without question, yet she moved to the nightstand to check the Caller ID, anyway. She stared at the familiar cell number, her anger snowballing with each incessant ring. Stupid jerk. Did he really think she'd be willing to talk to him at this point? Or ever?

Finally, the ringing stopped, and she exhaled slowly. Her gaze caught on the pretty pink tote bag sitting near her closet door, and a fresh wave of pain and anger swept over her. Fueled by a fury she didn't recognize, she grabbed the bag of sexy lingerie she'd bought a week ago. The impulsive purchase had been the only thought she'd given to the wedding. Ironically, the lingerie was to have been for the honeymoon. Because she'd so desperately wanted to light a fire under Dennis. Boring, straitlaced Dennis, who'd always seemed to prefer watching the news channel to cuddling with her.

With a whimper, she took the bag with her as she started yanking open dresser drawers. Why, she didn't know, because she doubted she'd find a pair of scissors. There was one in the kitchen and probably a pair in the laundry room, but she couldn't wait to cut up the stupid black lace teddy.

How many times had she reasoned with herself that Dennis simply wasn't the passionate sort? His kisses were tame, his sexual appetite bordering on nonexistent. Yet he'd been all over the blonde as if he was a starving man. Obviously Kate was the one lacking, the one he found inadequate.

She swallowed back a sob. Screw him. He wasn't worth a single tear.

The phone rang again, and without even checking to see who it was, she picked up the receiver and slammed it down. But before she got to the door, it rang again. Was he insane? Was he going to call all night? Her nerves couldn't take it. This time after she slammed it, she picked up the receiver again and laid it beside the phone. Clint and Joe used their cells more than the landline. She doubted they'd realize the phone was off the hook. She was the one who was going to go mad if she had to listen to the warning buzz another second.

The tote bag still clutched to her breasts, her gaze darted to the dresser. Her car keys. Hadn't she left them there? No, they were in her purse. She grabbed the brown leather strap and swung the bulky pocketbook over her shoulder. She had to get out of here. No one would miss her. Not until morning. The problem was, she didn't know where to go.

She hesitated at the door, her hand on the doorknob, her palm suddenly clammy.

Mitch. He'd be staying at his family's ranch alone tonight. Her breath caught in her throat. Could she really do that? Just show up? Her gaze lowered to the scrap of black lace lying in the tote bag, and she suddenly recalled their hug. She briefly closed her eyes and replayed how good his arms had felt around her, how close he'd held her. How fast he'd made her heart beat.

No, that's not what she wanted right now. Besides, he'd never considered her as anything other than a pesky kid sister, and the last thing her bruised ego needed was more rejection. She stiffened, her hold on the doorknob a death grip.

Except that wasn't how he'd held her.

There had been nothing casual about the way he stroked her back, and had started to cup her fanny. Mitch had physically reacted to her. And definitely not as little Katie Manning. The thought registered with shocking clarity. At the time she'd felt too guilty about Dennis to absorb what had happened, but she wasn't wrong.

She swallowed. Was she?

Before she lost her nerve, she opened her bedroom door, checked to be sure the coast was clear and slipped into the hall. If she hurried, she'd probably beat him back to his place.

IT HAD BEEN GOOD TO SEE Clint again, Mitch thought as he passed the detached garage and parked his pickup near the front door of the rambling old ranch house. The porch steps needed a few repairs and the whole front a new paint job, but considering the age of his family's place, it was still in pretty good shape. No thanks to him.

Mitch pushed away the guilt that had started to gnaw at him the moment he'd set eyes on the wooden sign that arched over the entrance to the ranch. Though his father had never once complained, Mitch knew that keeping the ranch operational for the past few years had been a struggle. Their longtime foreman had retired, and then Clarence, who'd been expected to take his place, had to step aside after injuring his back while dropping hay from the back of a pickup. Soon after, the rustlers had struck for the first time.

It was Mitch's sister who'd finally filled him in on the news. His parents hadn't bothered. Why should they? Hadn't they figured out long ago they couldn't count on their only son for help? That the only thing they could count on was for him to selfishly go his own way?

Exhausted suddenly, Mitch climbed out of the truck and headed for the front door. He'd driven ten hours straight yesterday, and another ten today with only a half hour stop to shovel in some fast food. Turned out he'd pushed hard for nothing. He'd missed the July Fourth celebration anyway. Probably just as well. Once again he'd been thinking about himself by wanting to use the gathering to talk to as many neighbors as possible. But the folks around here deserved a festive weekend without their thoughts being consumed by the rustling problem.

Just as he got to the porch steps he thought he saw a light flicker from the second floor. He stopped, his gaze scanning the darkened windows. The moon was full, and he decided that he must have seen a reflection off the glass. He'd stopped by earlier, long enough to take in his duffel bag and grab a quick shower. As he'd always done, he'd left the front door unlocked without giving the habit a second thought. Maybe he'd better start paying more attention.

He let himself in, then waited and listened. Enough moonlight shone in through the windows that he didn't need to turn on lights. He climbed the stairs, smiling at the familiar creaks. How many times had he been busted trying to sneak in after curfew because of these damn noisy stairs? More than he could count. Even his sister had gotten in trouble a night or two.

He stopped in the bathroom to brush his teeth before going to his old room. Now that he was six-one, he wasn't looking forward to sleeping in the double bed that had been perfectly fine until college. His parents had a king-size bed in the master bedroom that would be more comfortable, but the pull of his old room was too strong.

The moon's glow continued to provide enough light until he got to the end of the hall. His parents had left most of the furnishings, but surprisingly, he noticed the few missing pieces they had taken with them. As a kid he couldn't have cared less about the cherry table his father had painstakingly labored over for two winters or the grandfather clock his great-great-grandmother had brought with her from Germany, but their absence produced a pang of sadness he couldn't explain.

When he got to his room, he stopped short of flipping on the switch for the glaring overhead light. Instead, he used the moonlight to guide him to the lamp.

"Mitch?"

The soft voice startled him and he nearly knocked over the lamp. "Who the—Katie?"

"Yes."

He righted the lamp, found the switch and muted light flooded the room. Lying in his bed, the blue hand-made quilt drawn to her chin, she blinked and squinted at the invading glow of the lamp.

"Damn it, Katie, you scared the hell out of me."

Her mouth curved in a tentative smile. "I didn't think you were afraid of anything. You even worked as a bodyguard for that TV actress for a while, didn't you?"

"What are you doing here?"

Her lips thinned and she shrank back. "Waiting for you."

"In my bed?"

She blinked, uncertainty and embarrassment filling

her green eyes. And then she lifted her chin. "You want me to leave?"

Mitch stared at her, feeling more helpless than he had in a long time. His mind flashed back to the earlier scene at the bunkhouse. Obviously that's what this was about. She was hurting, and if he wasn't careful, he'd only make her feel worse. But this was Katie…in his bed. Shit. This was totally messed up.

"No, I don't want you to leave," he said finally.

She gave him a fleeting smile of relief, and then moistened her lips. "The front door was unlocked."

"Old habit. Maybe not such a good idea these days." Giving her his back, he walked to the dresser to toss his keys, feeling like a flustered fourteen-year-old.

"Probably not," she said, sounding wounded.

He realized what he'd said, how she had taken it, but he had no idea how to backtrack. Or move forward. What the hell was he supposed to do now? Remind her she was engaged? Yeah, that would go over real well. He tried to get a furtive glimpse of her in the mirror but the angle was wrong. What was she wearing? She had the quilt pulled so far up he couldn't tell. A succession of possibilities flitted through his head, the one of her totally nude shocking him back to reality.

He cleared his throat and slowly turned around to face her. "What's going on, Kate?"

She hesitated, and then calmly lifted the quilt and folded it back. "Just keeping your bed warm for you."

Black lace and bare creamy skin. Just this side of naked and as tempting as sin itself. All thoughts of her as his friends' skinny sister fled as he slowly traced the curves of her body. Everything about her was lush and inviting, and his cock hardened in response.

Somewhere deep in the recesses of his brain he knew he should look away. But he just stood there, mesmerized. The sight of her plump pink-crowned breasts sent his ache deep. Visible through the sheer black material, her nipples were large and budded. His whole body tensed. Man, he had a thing for large pink nipples. He could almost taste them. Hungered to roll his tongue over those tight nubs as he thrust into all that magnificent heat. He stepped forward, reminding himself he was invited.

Then he saw her hand tremble. He gave himself a mental shake, and moved back as he lifted his gaze to her face. "This isn't a good idea."

She blushed. "I'm not a kid anymore."

In spite of himself he glanced at her breasts. "No, you certainly aren't."

She looked pleased, and then her brows drew together in a frown. As if the thought had just occurred to her, she slowly asked, "Are you involved with anyone?"

"No." Too late he realized he should've lied.

"Good." Her attention shifted to below his belt.

No use trying to hide his erection, which only grew at her blatant stare. He had to do something now, stop this before he made a huge mistake. "I'm not involved, but you are."

Her eyes widened, flooding with hurt and humiliation, before she shuttered them. Her chin quivered, and she pulled the quilt back over her body. "Don't believe everything you hear."

A rush of fierce protectiveness hit him like a tidal

wave, sweeping away his common sense. She looked so crushed and vulnerable he wanted to go to her, hold her. But that could be a mistake. It wasn't that he didn't trust himself…

That was a lie, and he knew it. He shouldn't still be hard, knowing what she'd been through, but damn it, he was. He wanted her something fierce, almost enough to ignore his duty, their friendship.

Like the coward he was, he sat at the far edge of the bed.

"Look, Kate," he said quietly, clasping his hands together and putting his elbows on his knees. "I understand why you're hurt and angry. But the guy's obviously a jerk and isn't worth you doing something foolish that you'll regret later."

"Must I repeat that I'm not a kid anymore? As far as your patronizing tone—" She abruptly stopped, her expression guarded. "What did you mean? Why should I be hurt and angry?"

Mitch cursed himself. He tried to think of something quick to cover his slip, but he was at a total loss.

"Why do you think Dennis is a jerk? You haven't even met him." Suspicion clouded her face and she stared hard at him, as if looking for a clue.

He shrugged. "You two obviously had a fight."

She raised herself to one elbow, oblivious of the quilt slipping from her body. Her gaze stayed fixed on his until guilt got the better of him and he had to look away.

"You saw— Oh, no." Her words ended in a whimper. She shoved back the quilt, kicking it free of her legs and tried to crawl out of the bed. She managed to get one foot on the floor.

Mitch lunged and caught her around the waist. "Katie, wait."

"Let me go."

"Hear me out."

"You were right. This was a mistake. Please." Her voice caught. "I have to go."

He tightened his hold, bringing her quivering body to rest against his chest. Selfishly, he was glad he couldn't see her face. The pain he knew was there would tear him up inside. "Stay."

"I can't."

He settled back and drew her onto his lap. "I promise I won't touch you. I know you don't want to go back and face your brothers. You think I'm an insensitive idiot…"

A strangled laugh broke from her lips, and she sniffed. "I'm okay. Really."

"I'm not. What if the rustlers come back? You want to leave me here all alone?"

She twisted around to look at him, amusement gathering in her watery eyes. "You're a dope."

"Yep." He smiled and hugged her closer. "Stay the night. We can talk if you want to. I'm still your friend, Katie, and you shouldn't be alone. Stay."

3

"EXCUSE ME, but five minutes ago you asked me what the hell I was doing here." Kate tried to sound spunky but she sounded more like a whipped puppy.

Mitch chuckled. "Sorry, must be getting old. A beautiful woman wants my company and I fold just because I've been driving for two days."

She sighed. "Don't, please." She struggled to get off his lap, but his arms tightened around her.

"What did I say?"

"When I was twelve you could've patronized me and I still would've thought the sun rose and set on your ass. Fifteen years later, I've had enough of patronizing men, thank you very much."

He snorted. "Explain how I was patronizing." He sounded genuinely perplexed, and maybe even irritated.

She smiled sadly. "Okay, so maybe you are just being a nice guy. A friend. But honestly, you don't need to soothe my wounded ego, okay? I'm a big girl. Dennis is a creep, and I'll get over this." Amazing how saying his name managed to slice through her. She didn't love him. That truth had slowly revealed itself to her over the past couple of weeks, and then come to a head tonight. But his betrayal still hurt. Did he have no respect for her at all? Why hadn't she seen that?

If she weren't so exhausted, she probably would've had the good sense to have already changed out of this ridiculous outfit and sneaked back home and into her room before anyone knew she'd left. Glancing down at the skimpy black teddy, she winced. No matter what she'd thought, this had never been a good idea. As a cocky high school jock, Mitch had been out of her league even before he'd left town.

Since then, he'd worked as a personal trainer to the rich and famous, a bodyguard for a gorgeous TV star, and last Kate heard he'd gotten his pilot's license and now flew a private plane for a rich developer in Miami. She'd bet her brand-new SUV that the man had a beautiful young daughter who'd begged daddy to hire Mitch. He was simply one of those guys who women found charming, and no matter what, he'd always landed on his feet. And Kate was, both literally and proverbially, simply the girl next door.

Catching him off guard, she quickly pushed off his lap. Being cradled against him felt far too good, and even though she'd managed to keep the tears at bay, she didn't trust herself to remain composed.

"Kate." He caught her hand.

She stood there, wondering where she'd dumped her clothes, feeling terribly exposed. "Would you turn around, please?"

"Nope."

She turned to glare at him. "Mitch."

His gaze ran down the front of her, and she instinctively jerked her hand away and folded her arms over her chest. He cupped her waist and drew her closer. Then using one finger, he lightly stroked the upper curves of her breasts, where they plumped above the black lace and protection of her crossed arms.

She froze, barely able to breathe.

"You've turned into a beautiful woman, Kate. A very desirable woman. Don't think for one moment I wouldn't want you lying beneath me. But I'd be a bigger jerk than Dennis if I took advantage of you now." He lowered his hand, his gaze touching the tops of her breasts before meeting her eyes.

For a second, she had trouble finding her voice. The way he looked at her, she could almost believe that he found her desirable. Almost. "Like I said, you're a nice guy." To her astonishment, her eyes started to burn. Damn him. She'd been holding it together. She spun away from him, furtively swiping at an errant tear. "My clothes…I don't know where I left them…."

"Ah, Katie." He scooped her up from behind and carried her back to the bed. The gentle way he handled her renewed the threat of tears. She did her best to hide her face as he laid her down on the sheets. "Move over."

She felt like a big clumsy oaf trying to scoot her fanny to the other side, where the bed had been pushed up against the wall. He tucked the quilt around her body, and then sat at the edge of the mattress and pulled off his boots. Leaving on his clothes, he stretched out beside her on the small bed. He didn't try crawling under the sheets or the quilt, but punched the pillow under his head before giving her another look.

"You okay?"

She nodded, sincerely hoping her nose wasn't too horribly red. "This bed is too small for you as it is. I shouldn't—"

"Come here." He shifted, so that he could slip his arm under her neck and around her shoulders. He brought her close enough that she could lay her cheek on his chest. "Are you more comfortable?"

She hesitated, and then curled tentatively toward him. "Are you sure you—"

He reached to switch off the lamp and then picked up her arm and put it in a more comfy position around his waist. Giving her shoulders a light squeeze, he said, "I'm sure."

She smiled wryly. "You don't know what I was going to say."

"I figured you were going to tell me about that crush you had on me."

She gave a startled laugh and lifted her head. Moonlight washed in through the parted curtains and illuminated the amusement in his face. "What?"

He lightly kissed her hair and urged her to lie back down. "Let's see, how did you put it? You thought the sun rose and set on my ass."

"You're awful to bring that up. My admission was made in the heat of the moment. Besides, I was twelve."

"I'm fascinated because I had no idea."

"Are you serious?"

"I am."

Kate laughed. "I thought I was so pathetically obvious."

"Nope. You were such a tomboy, I figured you were just trying to keep up with Joe, Clint and me."

"Jeez. All that angst for nothing."

"So let me get this straight. You only had the hots for me when you were twelve and then it just disappeared?"

"Shut up."

Mitch chuckled. "I like the idea of being the coveted older man."

"As if you didn't have enough girls chasing after you. If I recall, the entire cheerleading squad drew straws to see who you and Clint would take to the prom."

"Right."

Along with the sarcasm, she thought she detected a hint of embarrassment in his voice, and she grinned. "Besides, I got over you by the time I went to college."

"Cast aside for those college hunks, huh?"

"I rarely saw you anymore."

The sudden tension radiating from his body put her on alert. Although the Colters never confided disappointment in their son's frequent absences, it had to be an issue. She was sorry to have brought it up.

They lay there in silence until she wondered if he'd fallen asleep. As exhausted as she was, she was suddenly keyed up. The mere act of lying here with Mitch was so surreal it was impossible to relax. Plus, she was wearing a teddy, for heaven's sake.

Darn it, why did she have to remember that? It shouldn't matter. The thick quilt was quite an effective barrier between them. The thought of the sheer black lace that did nothing to hide her breasts made her squirm anyway. This was so not her style.

He lightly squeezed her shoulders. "I thought you were asleep," he whispered.

"I thought *you* were."

"We both should be."

"Yeah." *Right.* She was snuggled against Mitch's broad strong chest. His rock-hard biceps held her a willing prisoner. Sure. She was going to get all kinds of sleep. "I have another confession."

He rested his chin on the top of her head. "Do I want to hear this?"

She smiled. "Probably not."

"You're going to tell me, anyway."

Kate wrinkled her nose, her courage slipping. It seemed funny a second ago, but maybe this was too much information. "Never mind," she murmured.

"Now I'm curious."

She nibbled her lower lip. "I used to kiss my pillow and pretend it was you."

He hooted with laughter. "How did I do?"

"You weren't bad."

"At least better than a bedpost, I suspect."

"Oh, much."

Mitch laughed again. "I'm not going to ask."

She lightly pinched his ribs. At least she tried. But he had no spare flesh. Just lean muscle that reminded her how near-perfect he was, and that she hadn't exercised since school let out last month. "Tell me you didn't practice kissing when you were a kid."

"I did my share, except it always involved a girl."

"Of course, silly me. You had them lining up."

"You have a warped sense of history, young lady."

Kate knew better, but she said nothing. If she were to pinch anyone, it should be herself. She was lying in bed with Mitch Colter. So he had on his clothes, and she was stiflingly swaddled like a newborn. It didn't matter that the AC was on, this was July and the evenings didn't cool down all that much. Normally she'd sleep with only a sheet covering her lower half. The heat from Mitch's body didn't help, either, or maybe it was her own rising temperature, but she had no intention of moving.

Her mind helplessly returned to Dennis. If it were him beside her, she wouldn't hesitate to put some distance between them or tactfully point out that it was too warm to be this close. Not that he'd ever been the physical type. The lack of affection had bothered her at first, but after a while she'd gotten used to it. In fact, she'd never been crazy about the way he kissed. Too stiff, too perfunctory. And damn it, kissing was important to her. So why had she been willing to overlook such a major flaw?

"Dennis was a lousy kisser," she muttered, for an instant uncertain whether she'd said that out loud, and then wishing she hadn't.

Mitch shifted slightly, his chin grazing her temple, but he didn't comment.

"Sorry, I guess I shouldn't be talking about him."

"Go ahead. I told you we could talk. Let it out."

She sighed. "Maybe it was me. Maybe I just wasn't…" She paused. This wasn't helping. She was still too raw to censor herself, and this wasn't the kind of conversation she wanted to have with Mitch.

"Wasn't what?" He almost sounded angry.

She'd clearly overstayed her welcome. First she'd barged in uninvited, and now she was depriving him of sleep. "I should go. It's late and neither of us is likely to get any rest."

"If we don't get to sleep, it's because it's too damn hot." He freed his arm and swung his feet to the floor.

She threw back the quilt, untangling her legs, and preparing to crawl around him. Facing him tomorrow was going to be a bear. But right now she only had to worry about getting to her car, which she'd parked in the back, in the dark. Crap.

"Hold on. I'm just taking off my shirt."

She swallowed, tempted to linger and get a good look at his naked chest. She rose before she changed her mind. "This is crazy. There's no reason for me to stay."

"Look, if you leave now, I'll have to follow you back to your ranch," he said, sounding weary. "Someone will hear us. Then Joe or Clint will come out and want to know what's going on. Is that what you want?"

"I live fifteen minutes away, in case you've forgotten. You're not following me back."

"You're not leaving unless I do." He unfastened the last button, and then met her eyes with irritating authority.

"Wanna bet?" She planted a hand on her hip, ready to do battle, but then he did something totally unfair.

He shrugged out of the shirt.

The moonlight hit him just right. Helplessly, she stared at the rippling muscles of his smooth chest, the way they flexed and relaxed with the flow of his movements as he tossed the shirt toward the oak chair in the corner.

When she finally lifted her gaze, she found that he was staring at her breasts through the sheer black teddy. His preoccupation made her feel marginally better. At least he hadn't caught her ogling him.

He blinked, briefly met her gaze and then pushed the quilt to the foot of the bed. "A sheet should be enough," he murmured.

"Enough for what?"

The question drew a crooked smile from him. "Get back in."

Kate pressed her lips together. She was enjoying this. No matter how small the chink in his armor, this was a human side to Mitch she'd never experienced. He'd always seemed controlled and in charge.

"Do I have to pick you up?" he asked with one arched brow.

"I thought you were afraid of bodily contact."

"Afraid, hell," he scoffed. "I'm terrified down to my little toes."

She grinned. He was being sweet, and she appreciated the gesture. "You know, there is a sensible solution. I could sleep in your sister's old room."

He hesitated, considering the possibility. "Too dusty. It took me half an hour to get this room ready." He yawned heartily. "How much longer are we going to argue about this?"

Disappointment dampened her spirits. She'd enjoyed the brief flirtation, but apparently she wasn't that irresistible. Like the good girl she'd always been, she crawled back into bed.

The truth was, she didn't want to have to talk to anyone else tonight. Or disrupt the whole house by trying to sneak back in this late.

The sheets were nice and cool compared to the heavy quilt. She slid between them, and then shrank close to the wall to give him as much room as possible.

After Mitch got in beside her, he pulled her back to lie on his chest again. But this time there was no fabric between her cheek and his smooth taut skin. She fisted her hand, afraid she might unconsciously grope him.

He stroked her back. "Am I crowding you?"

"No."

"Then relax," he whispered.

She thought he might have kissed the top of her head, but she wasn't sure. "I have one more question and then I promise I'll shut up."

"What's that?"

"Did you get a good look at her?"

His hand stilled; she missed the soothing motion. "Who?"

"The woman." She cleared her throat. "The blonde who was with Dennis."

"No," he said reluctantly.

"It happened so fast that I—" She couldn't seem to clear the obstruction in her throat. "I know she had blond hair, that's about all."

"Does it matter?"

"I guess not," she said softly.

"The guy is a friggin' dirtbag," Mitch said hotly. "And an idiot."

She smiled, knowing Mitch's fervor burned in her defense. "And a lousy kisser. That's quite unforgivable, actually."

Mitch caught her off guard by hooking a finger under her chin. As he forced her to look up, he tilted his own head back. "Any man who doesn't take the time to kiss you thoroughly isn't worth his salt."

She held her breath. Was he simply making a point or was he going to kiss her? At this angle she couldn't be sure, but she could feel the tension in his body, like a tiger restraining himself from pouncing on his prey.

He gently brushed his lips across hers. "You deserve

better, Kate," he said quietly. "You're pretty and smart and kind and—"

"A real girl next door, huh?" Her shoulders sagged. He wasn't going to kiss her. He was patronizing her again. "Guess the only way I'm ever going to light a fire is with a book of matches."

He chuckled. "And you have a sense of humor."

"Yeah, I'm hilarious."

"Ah, Katie, I am sorry about what happened tonight. But don't let that guy do this to you."

"Deep down I think I've known for a couple of weeks what I had to do, but I hadn't wanted to face it." Damn, but she had to stop trembling. "I probably owe Dennis a thanks. He saved me the trouble of having to call off the wedding myself. I always did have a knack for picking out the wrong men. I should just plain give it up."

MITCH STIFFENED. She wasn't thinking clearly, that was for certain. It wasn't like her to indulge in this kind of self-pity, even though she deserved to wallow. And here he'd been about to take advantage of her vulnerability. Hell, it was only going to be one kiss. Still, bad timing. But he knew she was feeling unwanted and unattractive, and it wasn't right. He hated that the ass had her second-guessing herself. A kiss from him wasn't going to fix that.

She'd get over the betrayal, since the Kate he remembered was too bright and sensible to let a man determine her worth. But it would take some time for the fog of pain to lift. In the meantime, the best thing he could do for her was be a friend.

"Mitch?" She was looking up at him, most of her face

in shadow, but the slight tremor in her voice told him more than he could read in her eyes. "Are you going to kiss me?"

He should've let her go, he realized. Urged her to leave the minute he'd arrived home. She'd be safely tucked away in her own bed right now, asleep, after having indulged in a cathartic crying jag. Then, tomorrow she could get on with the grieving process. Leave it to him to mess up everything.

Mitch kissed the tip of her nose, and then each eyelid.

He lowered his hand from her chin. "Get some rest, Kate," he said, before extricating his arm from beneath her shoulders. It wasn't easy but he rolled over, giving her his back and letting one arm dangle off the bed.

Best thing for everyone concerned was for him to stay the hell away from Kate Manning.

4

MITCH WAS STRETCHED OUT on the hardwood floor beside the bed when she woke. His pillow was beneath his head but he had no sheet or anything else to keep him comfortable. Kate winced, but there would be time later for kicking herself for being so self-centered. The muted dawn light coming through the window told her she had to get home fast. Never mind the embarrassment of facing Mitch in the light of day, her girlfriends would be leaving for the Houston airport soon.

Carefully, she crawled to the foot of the bed where she could avoid stepping on him. Suddenly, she remembered the pink tote—it held her clothes and it was sitting on the floor near the door. She tiptoed toward the bag, snatched it up and kept walking until she reached the bathroom. For all she knew, she'd awoken him, but she hadn't dared turn around. It wasn't even so much the skimpy black teddy barely covering her bottom that had her anxious to disappear, although that would probably haunt her later. It was the idea that she'd for even a mere second thought she could find comfort, or worse, validation in Mitch Colter's arms.

She slipped quietly into the bathroom and changed in record time, her skin clammy with the residual effects of a bad dream. The kind you wake up to and feel intense relief that the events hadn't been real. She should have reconsidered before coming here. The tequila couldn't be blamed for her poor judgment because she hadn't touched a drop. Yet her reckless actions had been atrociously akin to the time when one of the cowhands had come off a bender and deemed it smart to climb on a newly acquired wild mustang. He'd ended up breaking an arm and a leg. Maybe she should consider herself lucky. Then again, she might prefer broken bones to her shattered pride.

Fortunately, she made it out of Mitch's house, and back to the Sugarloaf without incident. Several men were out near the barn doing their morning chores, but the house was quiet, even the kitchen. Kate had given their housekeeper the week off after all the extra work she'd done for the party, so Kate started the coffee and then hurried upstairs to get out of last night's clothes and grab a shower.

The place was eerily quiet. Normally Joe and Clint would have been up already, eating a quick breakfast and slurping down coffee before they went outside to work. But Kate hadn't expected them to lapse into routine this morning. Not after hooking up with two of her friends over the weekend. Even Jessica, her third college roommate, had found an unlikely connection with Ben, a friend of the Manning family. How ironic that the three of them had come all the way to Texas to help her celebrate her engagement and each ended up finding someone.

Kate hated that she was jealous. But Dennis had never once looked at her the way Joe had gazed yearningly at Lisa last night. And the glorious way Clint made Dory smile…

It was more than Kate could think about without wanting to crawl back into bed and pull the covers over her head. She hurried with a minimum of makeup, mostly to hide the dark circles under her eyes, leaving her hair to dry by itself. It would end up wavy and too wild but she didn't care. After her friends left, she planned on hibernating for a week.

By the time she started downstairs, she still hadn't decided what to tell her friends. She didn't want their weekend to end on a bad note, yet they had to be wondering about what happened last night.

"Kate?"

She heard Dory's voice just as she entered the hall to the kitchen. Kate pasted on a cheerful face and turned to her friend. Jessica was directly behind Dory, both of them wearing concerned frowns.

"Good morning," Kate said brightly, and then burst into tears.

THE SUGARLOAF WAS BACK to normal. The tents were gone, the stage and booths already dismantled, only a few picnic tables and benches remained near the bunkhouse. Mitch had intended to help with the teardown and clean up, but he'd gotten up too late. He pulled his pickup off to the shoulder of the driveway and noticed Clint's truck parked near the barn. Good. Mitch was hoping to catch either him or Joe, preferably both of them.

As he climbed out of his pickup, his gaze went toward the house. Kate's small SUV was nowhere in sight but that didn't mean she wasn't home. She could have parked in the garage or on the other side of the house. He hoped it wouldn't be awkward when they saw each other later. That she'd skipped out while he was still asleep wasn't a total surprise, but he wished they could have talked first. He was totally okay with how last night had played out, but he had a feeling she wasn't.

Pete, one of the cowhands who'd been working for the Mannings for as long as Mitch could remember, waved him toward the barn. The tempting smell of coffee coming from inside was enough incentive.

"Good to see you again, Mitch," the old-timer said. "I thought I spotted you last night."

"Yep, I got here late. Wish I could've made it for the rodeo."

"Don't know if you heard, but Ben didn't ride yesterday. Got himself a spinal fracture and had to quit rodeoing. The doc said if he gets thrown one more time it could do him in."

"I found out last night." He'd felt badly about the news and looked for Ben. They'd known each other since kindergarten. "Too bad his career got cut short, but at least he had enough sense to call it quits."

Nodding, Pete raised his mug. "I reckon you're looking for Joe and Clint, but there's a fresh pot of coffee brewing inside if you've got a mind to take a cup."

"Come on, Pete. Have I ever turned down your coffee?"

The gray-haired man chuckled, and Mitch followed him inside, noticing the slight stoop to his shoulders and how he favored his right leg. The eight years since he'd last seen Pete hadn't been kind to the older man. Mitch thought about his own father, trying to keep the ranch afloat with only two hired hands for help. Granted, he was a good ten years younger than Pete, but that knowledge didn't dull the stab of guilt.

The inside of the barn had hardly changed. A large assortment of tack was neatly arranged on the left wall, dozens of bales of hay were stacked between the horse stalls and two rows of saddles. In the corner was a shed. That was new. Not so the smells. The musky scent of sweat mingled with leather and hay was as familiar as the packed dirt beneath his boots.

By the time Mitch filled a mug with the strong black brew that Pete was famous for, he heard Clint's and Joe's voices as they entered the barn. They both wore new jeans and Western-cut shirts, instead of the usual faded work Levi's jeans and T-shirts. Joe looked as if he might even have polished his boots.

The old-timer obviously noticed Mitch's surprise because he leaned over and whispered, "Them boys are in love." Cackling to himself, he strode past Joe and Clint on his way out of the barn.

Joe saw Mitch first and extended his hand as he approached. "Clint told me you were here last night. Sorry I missed you, buddy."

"I hit a lot of traffic outside of Dallas and got here late. But I'll be staying awhile." He shook Clint's hand, too, even though he'd seen him briefly last night. "What are you two all gussied up for?"

"We just got back from the airport," Joe said, glancing at Clint. "Kate's friends had flights to catch."

"They must be mighty-fine-looking friends."

Clint grinned.

Joe rubbed his jaw, looking uncharacteristically sheepish.

Mitch guessed the old-timer was on to something. "Where's Kate? Didn't she go with you?"

Clint frowned. "Kate? No, why?"

Mitch tensed. "They are her friends."

"We kind of wanted to see them off, and anyway she had a headache. Look, I'm going to go change." Joe clapped him on the shoulder. "Have you eaten?"

"Thanks, but I have to run into town," Mitch said absently, his mind on Kate. Clearly she hadn't told her brothers about Dennis yet. Mitch hadn't expected her to mention his role last night, but he was still relieved to know that her brothers had been kept in the dark. "Before I go I wanted to ask you about the new sheriff."

"He's not that new. Been in office over a year now. For the most part folks have been fairly happy with the job he's done." Clint poured himself a cup of coffee. "I expect you want to talk to him about the rustling."

Mitch nodded, and Clint and Joe exchanged concerned looks.

"I can change later," Joe said grimly. "Why don't we go sit in the kitchen and talk?"

Something about the way Joe had lowered his voice made Mitch uneasy. There were a couple of cowhands working near the stalls. Did Joe suspect their own men of being involved? Or had the situation deteriorated to the point that no one knew who to trust? Then, too, Mitch wasn't anxious to go to the house and run into Kate. Not in front of her brothers.

"I didn't mean to ambush you. I'm going to be around awhile. This can wait."

"Now is as good a time as any." Joe passed a weary hand over his face. "I'm still tired from the weekend. It's not like I'm gonna get much done today."

"Amen." Clint drained his coffee. "Let's go."

Mitch had little choice but to follow their lead, and hoped like hell Kate was locked away in her room. Though he had a feeling she'd do her best to stay clear of him, too.

After walking the modest distance under the broiling sun to the house, they all decided they'd had enough coffee. Clint got a pitcher of iced tea out of the refrigerator, while Joe brought out glasses and set them on the kitchen table. As he'd done hundreds of times before, Mitch sat at the familiar oak table with his two friends, and damn if it didn't feel like only weeks had passed instead of years.

"Where's Ben?" he asked. "He hasn't left yet, has he?"

"He had some business in Dallas, and then he was going to head up to look at some land in the panhandle." Clint removed his hat and hung it off the back of a spare chair. "He'll be back in a couple of weeks."

Mitch figured he hadn't worn his Stetson in ten years. He hoped it was still in his closet. "How's he doing? Having to quit rodeoing had to be quite a blow."

"I think he's still in shock." Clint shook his head. "The dummy wanted to ride one last time yesterday. Good thing one of Kate's friends talked him out of it."

Mitch felt for Ben. Hard enough to be forced to give up something you love, worse when it happens when you're at the top of your game. "I'm glad I'll get to see him."

"So you are sticking around for a while then?" Joe unsnapped his cuffs and rolled them back.

"For as long it takes to find out what's going on with these rustlers."

Clint snorted. "They're sneaky cowards. After they

strike they lie low long enough for everyone to think they've moved on, then bam, they move in again."

"You guys haven't had any trouble, have you?" Mitch asked.

"None." Joe shook his head. "They only seem to be hitting the smaller, lower-tech ranches. Except for the Double R. Frank Reynolds got slammed twice by them. He lost so many cattle the second time that he had to let half his men go. Friday night he told me he might have to sell off his north pasture just to make payroll and supplement whatever herd he has left."

A sickening thought occurred to Mitch. "Anything happen over the weekend?"

"No, Joe and I brought in extra security from Houston and made sure guards were posted at all the ranches," Clint said. "We figured the long weekend would be open season with most folks attending the festivities here."

The Mannings' generosity didn't surprise Mitch. They were busy running the second-largest ranch in the county, yet they'd always looked out for their neighbors. "Shouldn't the sheriff have taken care of that?"

"It's only him and two deputies," Joe said, shrugging. "They can only do so much. As it was, neither Chuck Jackson or Lou Davis came with their families to the party this year. They were too afraid to leave their property even with the extra guards."

Mitch grudgingly acknowledged that the sheriff could cover only so much territory. He still didn't like the man.

Clint studied Mitch thoughtfully. "Have you met the sheriff yet?"

"No, I talked to him on the phone. But he sure was one uncooperative son of a gun."

Clint frowned. "Can't account for that. He seems to be a fairly straight shooter. Nobody's complained about him, anyway."

"Look how long this has been going on, and he has no leads?" Mitch grunted. "You'd think he would've asked for outside help by now."

"You have a point," Joe agreed. "Though there hasn't been an incident since beef prices dropped. Which makes sense since typically that's when rustling cools down."

"Yeah, but that doesn't help the victims who've already been chased off their ranches." Mitch's bitterness rang through loud and clear. "Matter of fact, I just didn't like the sheriff's attitude when I called. I hope he's not an ass in person."

"Want me to go to town with you?" Clint offered.

Mitch half smiled and pushed back from the table. "I promise not to raise any hell."

KATE WOULD HAVE MUCH preferred to shut herself in her room for the day, but from her bedroom window she saw Mitch's truck coming down the driveway and knew she had to leave. Joe and Clint would probably invite him to dinner later, and she was far from ready to face him even then. Especially not in front of her brothers. For a minute she considered stretching out her headache excuse if they tried to get her to go downstairs, but eventually she concluded she'd be better off leaving.

After scribbling a note that she'd gone to town and leaving it in the den, she sneaked out the patio door near where she'd parked her car last night. If her brothers and Mitch heard her leave, she didn't care, though she doubted they would be able to all the way from the barn.

As soon as she got to the highway she switched on her cell phone, annoyed to see that she had four messages from Dennis. She didn't want to worry her brothers by being unreachable. Dennis, on the other hand, could get lost. She still hadn't talked with him since last night, nor had she told Clint and Joe that the wedding was off. Naturally, they'd want to know what happened, and she doubted they'd settle for her claiming irreconcilable differences.

If she told them the truth, they'd likely go kick Dennis's ass. As much as he'd deserve it, the humiliation factor for her to admit that he cheated squashed that option.

She arrived in town in record time, which meant she had to have been speeding like crazy. The scary thing was that she had no recollection of how fast she'd driven. After parking in front of Wilbur's Food Town, she sat numbly in the car. Her head felt heavy from lack of sleep and from the frank and emotional conversation she'd had with her friends before they'd left this morning. They had all wanted to run Dennis up a flagpole. She really should have let them.

She was about to get out of the car when her cell rang. Certain it was Dennis, she nearly ignored it, but relented in case it was Joe or Clint. It was Lisa, who was supposed to be in the air by now, and Kate quickly answered before the call went to voice mail.

"Where are you?" Kate asked by way of greeting. "Was your plane delayed?"

"I'm just landing in Chicago."

Kate stared at her watch, trying to make sense of how much unaccountable time had passed since she'd hugged her friends goodbye.

"I guess Joe didn't tell you. I almost missed my flight. Got on just before they closed the doors."

"I haven't seen him or Clint."

"Okay, that answers my next question." Lisa paused. "When are you going to tell them the wedding is off?"

"I don't know. Soon, though. Dennis keeps calling, but I know *he* won't say anything, the coward."

"I guess you haven't seen Mitch, either."

Kate sighed. She really hadn't meant to tell the girls about him, but everything had sort of tumbled out. "No, and I don't plan to for the rest of my life."

Lisa chuckled, and then her voice lowered soothingly. "How are you doing, kiddo?"

"I'll live."

"Where are you?"

"In town. I have a few errands to run."

"Perfect. Listen up—I have some homework for you."

Kate groaned. No telling what Lisa would suggest. Even when they were in college Lisa was bold and confident, sometimes rather colorful. Now, as a well-known Chicago reporter, her assertive, take-no-prisoners style had earned her several awards.

"First, no groaning. I want you to— You do have a department store around there, don't you?"

"Kind of."

"Do they have sexy clothes?"

"Oh, no." Kate shook her head. "I am not—"

"Okay, not sexy, but something the old Kate Manning would never think of wearing."

"I did that last night, remember?" Kate said flatly.

"Huh? You left that part out. Listen," Lisa rushed on, "I have to deplane any second, so listen. This isn't about Mitch. This is about you stepping out of your comfort zone. Shaking off the old and stepping into the new. Got it?"

"Sure."

"I'm serious. Has playing it safe worked for you?"

Kate sighed. She loved Lisa, she did. But Lisa didn't understand.

"I'm not trying to be mean, Kate. I'm trying to help." Lisa muttered a mild oath. "I have to go. But I'll call you later. Chin up, kiddo."

Kate scarcely got out her goodbye and the call was disconnected. Oddly, she felt somewhat better, energized even. Not that she was going to follow Lisa's crazy suggestion, but it felt as if some of Lisa's confidence had rubbed off.

She climbed out of the car, intent on returning the blanket that Thelma, the cashier at Wilbur's Food Town, had forgotten last night. Kate slowed as she rounded the hood of the car, catching a glimpse of the strappy red sundress in Porter's Sport and Sundry display window. It wouldn't hurt to poke around inside, she supposed. Not that she'd ever wear something so low-cut like that in public. Dennis would have a heart attack.

Kate didn't hate that idea.

5

MITCH HAD DECIDED TO TAKE a chance that the sheriff would be in his office, instead of warning the man that he was coming into town. Clint and Joe had no quarrel with the lawman so Mitch didn't know what his problem was. Maybe he'd caught the guy on a bad day when he'd phoned last week. But he didn't think so. The sheriff had been defensive and deftly evaded Mitch's questions to the point that he had felt compelled to make the trip home.

When he pulled to the curb across from the office, he was glad to see both the sheriff's car and one of the deputy's SUVs parked in front. He slid out from behind the wheel, while taking in the familiar storefronts that had lined Main Street since he was a kid. Nothing had changed. Not even the faded sign hanging over the barbershop touting hot shaves, or the one outside the tiny bakery offering cinnamon buns on Saturdays and Sundays only.

Someone could blindfold him and he'd know that Mildred's Fabric Shop was on one side of Wilbur's Food Town and Porter's Sundry on the other. The brick post office and bank sat side by side, and the gas station located at the other end of town probably still sold the best beef jerky for five hundred miles.

He'd bet the Corvette he had sitting back in Miami that every single man and woman over twenty-one still congregated at Barney's Bar and Grill on Friday and Saturday nights to shoot pool and inhale pitchers of beer. That is, if they didn't drive the extra thirty miles to Willowville, where they had an honest-to-goodness department store, a chain supermarket and a bar whose owner wasn't too picky about high school boys' fake IDs.

Only two cars passed before he trotted across the street. Someone from the rickety blue pickup waved. He couldn't see who it was but he automatically waved back. It didn't matter if he knew them or not, though he probably did.

The late-afternoon sun was brutal, and he welcomed the blast of cold air as he opened the office door. A younger man with a narrow face looked up from the computer screen he'd been concentrating on, and frowned at Mitch.

"Can I help you?" he asked.

"I hope so. Is the sheriff in?" Mitch looked past him and the other unoccupied desk toward the closed door to the inner office.

"Who's asking?"

"Are you the deputy?"

"One of 'em."

"I'm Mitch Colter. I spoke to Sheriff Harding last week. I might have spoken to you, too," he said, hoping the admission wasn't a mistake that would make the trip to town a waste of time. "I didn't catch your name."

"Deputy Barns," he said, looking put out. "You must've talked to Morton, not me." He pushed away from his desk, a tan, ill-fitting uniform hanging from his thin frame. "I'll check on whether the sheriff can see you."

While Mitch waited, he glanced around the office, which, again, had changed little since he'd last sat on the hard wooden bench near the door that led to the two cells in the back. He and Clint, both in high school at the time, had been picked up for speeding and possession of two empty beer cans. Being a good friend of the Mannings sure had its perks. They'd both gotten off with only a stern lecture.

The shuffle of feet drew his attention, and he turned to see a fortyish man with sagging jowls and thinning hair emerge from the office. He was tall and broad, and if Mitch wasn't mistaken, walked with a slight limp.

"What can I do for you, Mr. Colter?" he asked, hooking his thumbs in his belt, his voice cool and emotionless.

Mitch politely extended his hand. He hoped he was wrong about the bad vibe he'd gotten. "Nice to meet you in person, Sheriff Harding."

The man's slight hesitation didn't bode well for a friendly chat. He accepted Mitch's handshake, and then still unsmiling, inclined his head toward the coffeepot sitting on a metal filing cabinet. "Coffee?"

"No, thanks."

"Let's go in my office."

With avid interest, the deputy watched them until the sheriff closed the door behind Mitch.

The sheriff waited until they both sat facing each other across his cluttered desk and said, "I believe I know why you're here. What I don't think is that I can help you."

Mitch shrugged. "All I want is a little information."

"I gave you everything I could on the phone."

"Which was basically nothing."

The man's dark eyes narrowed. "This is an ongoing investigation. I'm limited in what I can divulge."

Mitch coolly surveyed the man, forcing himself to hold on to his temper. The guy obviously planned on stonewalling him. "Have you made any headway at all? Have you brought in any help?"

"You think I can't do my job?"

"This is a big county, Sheriff. Lots of territory to cover. There are only three of you. That's all I'm saying."

"Just so happens I'm thinking about hiring another deputy."

Mitch gritted his teeth. The guy couldn't be that myopic.

"And you think one more man will make a difference?"

"Look, Colter, I'm sorry about your family's ranch, I am. But the truth is, we haven't had another incident in three months. In my opinion, those fellas are long gone by now. I heard from the sheriff in Lerner that they had two ranches hit a month ago. Could be those were our boys heading north."

"So you've stopped investigating?"

"I didn't say that." Irritation creased his face. "I'm just saying that we don't have any new clues. Look, with everyone at the Mannings' shindig this weekend, it would've been the perfect opportunity for another strike, but nothing happened."

"You do know that Joe and Clint provided extra security for their neighbors."

"Yeah, I know," he said gruffly. "Would've been better if they hadn't. We were ready for a raid. Could've caught them red-handed."

"Thought you were convinced the rustlers moved north?"

The sheriff couldn't hide his anger. There was a flush climbing his beefy neck, and he glared at Mitch. "I don't like some outsider coming in here and questioning my competence. It's time for you to leave."

"Yep, you're right. No need to waste my time any longer." Mitch got to his feet, and then strode to the door. "Wish I could say it was a pleasure, Sheriff."

Mitch left the office before the man could respond, but before he made it outside, Harding came after him.

"Leave it alone, Colter. I catch you getting in our way, I will arrest you."

His hand on the doorknob, Mitch slowly turned around. The deputy's eyes nearly bugged out of his head as he glanced back and forth between Mitch and the sheriff. Mitch smiled and gave a slow disingenuous nod. "Don't worry, Harding. Like you said, those rustlers are probably long gone."

"HELLO, KATE, WHAT ARE YOU doing here? I thought you'd be sleeping for a month after all the commotion at your place this weekend." Marjorie Meeks set her tray of empty glasses on the bar and wiped her palms on her apron.

"I had to come into town so I figured I'd return things that were left from the picnic last night." She opened the plastic sack and let the waitress peer inside. "This is your casserole dish, I believe."

"That's it. That chip in the corner has been there since before I inherited the dish from my mama." Marjorie took the bag from Kate and set it on the bar. "You haven't been in here in ages. How about an iced tea? Or maybe you'd like Barney to fry you up a burger and onion rings? On the house."

Kate started to decline. The place was busy, mostly the bar area and the three pool tables in the adjoining room.

"Come on, honey. Those boys won't bite," Marjorie said, winking. "They aren't too liquored up yet."

Kate smiled. The last thing she was worried about was a bunch of cowhands, especially since she knew most of them. Half the men around the pool tables worked at the Sugarloaf, and if anything, they generally treated her like an eighty-year-old matron. "I'll take the iced tea, but only if you're not too busy."

"Nah, I called Ashley in when I saw how busy we were getting. The boys caught me by surprise. I didn't think so many of them would be coming into town after all the hoopla over the weekend."

"Clint and Joe are a bit slow moving themselves so I think they gave the men half a day off to recuperate."

Barney yelled from the back that an order was ready, and Marjorie rolled her eyes at her husband's booming voice. "I'll be right back with your tea."

"No hurry." Kate slid onto a stool and glanced around. She couldn't remember the last time she'd stopped in. Usually when she came into town it was to pick up some groceries Maria might have forgotten.

Besides, she knew that a lot of Sugarloaf employees frequented the place and she didn't want to cramp their style. Which, she feared, she was doing right now. Only two men she vaguely knew sat at the other end of the bar, and they paid her no attention, but a few shooting pool looked rather ill at ease, glancing frequently in her direction.

She wouldn't be rude. Once Marjorie returned with

her tea, she'd take a few sips and then pretend she'd forgotten an appointment.

"Hey, Kate." Ashley emerged from the kitchen and went straight to filling a pitcher with beer. "Great party this weekend. Thanks."

Kate shook her head in awe. "Marjorie mentioned she'd called you into work but—" Kate's surprised gaze went to the foaming pitcher. "Since when are you old enough to serve beer?"

Ashley laughed. "Please. I'm like almost twenty-two already. Time to start using my mom's heavy-duty night cream."

"Oh, yeah. Right. Don't make me hurt you."

The young blonde giggled. "Be right back."

Kate watched her sashay over to the guys playing pool, the pitcher on her tray, her jeans and V-neck T-shirt both so tight it was amazing the seams hadn't split. Some of the men stood back to let her pass, eyeing her from behind and exchanging glances amongst themselves. Kate promptly looked away, and then sneaked a sidelong look in their direction and watched Ashley flirt shamelessly with her customers.

God, but Kate envied her lack of inhibition. There was nothing tawdry or cheap in the way she interacted with the men. Her flirting was actually good-natured and harmless, but it was the effortless sexuality that was as much a part of Ashley as her blond hair and blue eyes that made Kate wistful. The waitress reminded her of Lisa. Kate could never be like them. Not in a hundred years.

And certainly not because she'd bought that stupid red sundress. After she drank her iced tea, she was going right back to Porter's and exchange it for something more sensible.

"Hey, Kate." Ashley returned, set her tray down and leaned a hip on the bar. "The guys want to know if you'd be interested in a game of pool."

Kate blinked. "What?" She didn't dare look over there, but instead, forced a laugh. "They're only kidding around."

"I don't think so," Ashley said in a singsong voice. "At least not Brad. He's the cute one with the long dark hair who works over at the Double R."

The invitation had been a token one, of course. Kate dared to sneak a peek. Brad touched the brim of his hat and gave her a sexy smile.

"Go," Ashley said, grinning. "I know you have a pool table at home. I'd like to see you whip their smug asses."

Kate swallowed. If she didn't know any better, she'd swear Lisa had called Ashley and put her up to this.

Ashley gave her a gentle push. "One game isn't going to kill you. I'll bring you a shot and a beer."

MITCH LEFT HIS TRUCK where it was and strolled down Main Street. The smell of grilling burgers and onions made his stomach growl, and he decided he'd much prefer Barney's cooking to his own for dinner. Clint had suggested he return to the Sugarloaf later to help them get rid of the leftover barbecue ribs and chicken, but he had a feeling that Kate wouldn't appreciate his presence.

Surprised at the number of cars and trucks parked outside for a Tuesday, he entered the dimly lit bar and burger joint to raucous laughter coming from the spare room where Barney had installed pool tables the year

Mitch had left for college. So much for a quiet dinner while he mulled over his next move.

"Bring her another one, Ashley," a man called out.

"No, don't. I'm serious. This is my last one."

At the sound of the familiar voice, Mitch turned in disbelief toward the pool tables…the exact moment that Kate tilted back her head and drained a shot glass of light amber liquid. She coughed, used the back of her wrist to wipe her mouth and then started laughing.

A tall cowboy with longish hair, who Mitch didn't recognize, sidled up to her. He smiled and handed her a pool cue, his other hand lingering at her waist.

"Thanks, Brad," she said, smiling up at him. "But in spite of the tequila, I do plan on beating you again."

"You can try, darlin', but I better warn you, I was just being polite that last game."

"Really?" She reared her head back, color high on her cheeks. "Then you wouldn't mind making a wager?"

The cowboy's mouth curved in a cocky smile. "Well, now, I suppose that could make things interesting."

Hell. She'd played right into his hands. Mitch knew that line too well. "Kate?"

She turned to look at him, her lips parting in surprise. "Mitch. Hi."

He scanned the other men's faces, recognizing a couple from the Sugarloaf. They'd shrunk away from the table and seemed as uncomfortable as he was with Kate's uncharacteristic behavior.

"I didn't know you were in town, Kate," he said easily as he strode over and insinuated himself into the small crowd. "Staying long?"

Her chin went up slightly, just enough to let him know he'd better tread lightly. "I don't know yet."

He couldn't tell if she was drunk. He didn't think so, but he also didn't think she needed another shot of tequila. "If you're sticking around, maybe you'd like to have dinner with me."

The cowboy she'd called Brad snorted and started to say something, but Kate interrupted. "I'll probably leave after this next game." The look she gave Mitch warned him not to push.

"All right," Mitch said. "I'll be at the bar if you change your mind."

He didn't miss her look of resentment as he left and headed for the bar, which gave him a bird's-eye view of the pool tables. Purposely he took the seat at the far end where the counter curved toward the wall. At that angle, he faced them head-on.

"What can I get ya?" the big-boned redhead asked, and he recognized Marjorie Meeks immediately. It took her a moment, and then she grinned. "Mitch Colter?"

He smiled back. "How are you and Barney doing, Marjorie?"

She chuckled. "It used to be Mrs. Meeks. Now you're all grown-up and calling me Marjorie." She walked away, and for an instant he thought he'd offended her. But then he saw that she'd left her post behind the bar and was coming toward him. "You give me a hug, young man."

Mitch rose from the stool and nearly got the life choked out of him. He hugged her back, and then patiently waited while she held him at arm's length and sized him up.

"Look how tall and handsome you are." She squeezed

his biceps. "All that hard muscle, too. You must have a missus by now."

"Not me."

"We'll just have to change that, now, won't we?"

Mitch laughed. "I don't think so."

She sniffed. "That's right. I heard you've been rubbing elbows with them Hollywood starlets and rich people."

"Sometimes," he admitted carefully. So far he'd escaped being tabloid fodder, and he meant to keep it that way. Then too, the lady involved had a right to her privacy, as well. "Only when the job calls for it."

"Order up," Barney hollered from the kitchen.

Marjorie sighed like a woman who'd been married to the same man for thirty years. "He'll want to come out and shoot the bull with you when he's caught up. I gotta go deliver my food to the table." On her way toward the kitchen, she gestured to the young blond waitress. "Ashley, get Mitch a beer on me."

She slipped behind the bar, her gaze narrowed on him. "Bottle or tap?"

"Tap is fine." He transferred his gaze to Kate, who was bending to take a shot. Brad was leaning back with his elbows on the windowsill and staring at her ass. Mitch's blood pressure rose, and he had to remind himself that Kate was a big girl, and it was none of his business.

"You're Mitch Colter, right? You played football with my older brother."

He broke from his trance and met the woman's blue eyes.

She smiled and set the frosty mug in front of him. "I'm Ashley Lambert."

"Ah, Jerry. We played during our junior and senior year. He still live around here?"

"Nope. Moved to Dallas with his wife and two kids."

Mitch nodded, only half listening while she continued to chat, his mind still on Kate. He tried not to stare by dividing his attention between Ashley and the pool players. But all he really wanted to do was scoop Kate up, take her to his truck and give her a good talking-to. He knew she was still reeling from last night, but he also knew that she would regret her behavior later if she continued flirting with Brad.

In the middle of her chattering, Ashley uttered the word *rustling,* and snagged his full attention.

"Did your family's ranch get hit?" he asked.

"What? Oh, no. I was just saying that I'm glad those creeps seem to have moved on." She glanced toward the pool players. "Everybody's been real edgy. Two of my daddy's wranglers just up and quit."

Mitch frowned. "Before or after the last assault?"

"I know what you're thinking, but they weren't involved. We knew them for a long time."

Which could mean nothing. "Did the sheriff talk to them?"

Ashley shrugged. "I doubt it." She leaned over the bar, her gaze drawn to the pool tables. One of the younger cowboys caught her eye and winked. "At least we've gotten some new blood around here," she said, grinning.

Mitch scanned the unfamiliar young faces. Any ambitious enough to join a rustling ring? "Do you know them all?"

"Sure. You probably know some of them. They've been around since I was a kid." She gestured with her

chin. "Brad and Seth sitting in the corner hired on at the
Double R last month. My daddy says it's not like it
used to be when cowhands stayed a lifetime. Lots of
drifters these days."

Mitch caught Brad staring at them. Unflinchingly
the guy met Mitch's eyes, the gleam of challenge un-
mistakable. Was that about Kate? Or something else?
Probably one of those cocky bastards who had to be the
only rooster in the henhouse.

Patting his pockets, Brad sauntered toward them.
"Ashley, darlin', how about getting us another round?"

"Sure thing."

"Put it on my tab and after I get my smokes from the
truck, I'll settle up with you." He nodded at Mitch, and
then headed for the door.

"Hmm." Ashley had already started filling a pitcher
with beer and getting out shot glasses. "Settling up early.
He must have a hot date."

As long as it wasn't with Kate, Mitch thought as he
took a long pull of beer and stared at the guy's retreating back. The funny thing was, from the nod, Mitch was
left with the distinct feeling that Brad was backing off.
But that didn't make sense. No matter. Mitch wasn't
about to let Kate out of his sight.

BRAD GOT TO HIS TRUCK, patted his pockets again and
glanced around to see if anyone was watching. Confident he was alone, he unlocked the truck, slid behind the
wheel and closed the door. The heavily tinted windows
shielded his privacy as he got out his cell phone and hit
speed dial. While he waited for the connection, he rifled
through his glove compartment for the half pack of cig-

arettes he kept there for an excuse to disappear when need be.

"Hey, it's me," he said, squinting toward the door of the bar. "Looks like we got a problem." He waited calmly for the cursing on the other end to stop. "Yep. Mitch Colter."

6

MITCH WORE FADED JEANS, boots, a crisp white shirt and a look of cool self-possession, which he once again turned on her. Kate looked away.

So now he was spying on her? Had Joe or Clint sent him to look for her? No, they wouldn't do that. Besides, they didn't know about her breaking up with Dennis, so they had no reason to worry. This was all Mitch's doing. Kate had a good mind to put on a show for him. Really give him something to stew over. Except if she went overboard, the whole town would talk, be wondering what had gotten into her.

Eventually they'd hear about her broken engagement, figure that was the reason for her acting out, and the pitying looks would start. No way could she abide that ordeal. It wasn't worth it. But one thing was for sure…she wasn't taking that dress back to Porter's now. The next time she came to town, she'd wear the stupid thing if it killed her. Everyone was so accustomed to seeing her in jeans, they'd probably still whisper, but so what.

She pretended to be interested in Brad positioning his cue to tap the nine ball, while she kept an eye on Mitch. She wanted to be sure he saw her have this last shot of tequila. Not that she had to worry. He'd been staring at her the entire time he'd been sitting at the bar. Wait till she got him alone. He was going to see a whole new side of her.

"You're up," Brad said.

She blinked, annoyed that she'd zoned out. She chalked her cue, and then neatly sank the eight ball. Game over. She'd won again.

"Damn." Brad shook his head. "You're amazing."

"Why, thank you." She picked up her shot of tequila and tossed it back. It burned all the way down her throat and pooled like fire in her empty stomach, but she kept a smile in place.

Brad set down his cue and grabbed his Stetson. "Well, I've been beaten up enough for one day. Time to go back to the bunkhouse and lick my wounds."

Kate grinned. "Don't feel bad. I beat Clint all the time, although he probably wouldn't admit it."

"Ah, hell, that was a low blow, darlin'," Brad said with mock irritation. "He beat me last week."

The rest of the guys started giving Brad the business, which he took with good-natured gruffness while he set his hat on his head. She liked him now when he wasn't being cocky. Interestingly, she'd had a good time this afternoon.

"You realize I'm going to have to restore my reputation," he told her. "I'm up for a game anytime you want."

"Oh, I don't know." She grabbed her purse. "I kind of like being the standing champ."

His mouth curved in one of those smug grins, and then he surprised her with a quick peck on the cheek. "See you, Kate."

Her gaze automatically sought Mitch's reaction. Brad walked out the door and she wasn't even sure she'd said goodbye. She was too busy watching Mitch head straight for her.

She quickly looked away, and addressed the remaining pool players with a bright smile. "Thanks for letting me play, gentlemen."

She didn't wait for the chorus of well-meaning platitudes but hurried for the door. Two of the men at the next table were Sugarloaf employees, and although she didn't expect Mitch to make a scene, anything he might have to say to her and vice versa was best done in private.

"Kate."

Halfway to the door she hesitated, when out of the corner of her eye, she saw Marjorie watching them. Kate exhaled slowly and faced him.

He studied her with annoying intensity. "The dinner offer still stands."

"No, thanks."

"Then how about a ride home?"

"I have my own car."

"Should you be driving?" he asked quietly.

"I'm fine." She wasn't lying. At least she didn't think so. "I really haven't had that much to drink."

"A couple of beers can hit a person who doesn't indulge much."

"And you know that about me how?" She shouldn't let him get to her, but he was aggravatingly right. "I might put away a six-pack a night, for all you know."

That he was obviously trying to control a smile annoyed her further. "I don't understand why you're so upset with me. I'm not the one who left this morning without a word."

She darted a look toward Marjorie. "Why don't you take an ad out in the paper?"

"Relax. No one heard." He did smile now. "Except the part that you put away a six-pack a night."

She gritted her teeth, trying to think of something clever to say when she heard the door open behind her. The sudden alertness in his eyes made her turn around. It was Sheriff Harding and his deputy.

"Good evening, Ms. Manning." The sheriff tipped his hat to her, and the deputy followed suit.

Evening? "Hello, Sheriff, Andy." Her gaze went to the window, and then to her watch. Good heavens, it was almost six-thirty.

Sheriff Harding looked past her, a hard glint in his eyes. "Still in town, Colter?"

Kate blinked. She hadn't had many dealings with the sheriff but he'd always been pleasant. Besides, how did he know Mitch?

Mitch let out a humorless laugh. "Is there a curfew I don't know about?"

The sheriff shrugged his beefy shoulders. "I just hope you're not asking questions better left to me."

The small crowd in the pool room had gotten quiet. Although it was unlikely they could hear the exchange, the sudden tension in both rooms was thicker than Barney's country gravy.

Mitch smiled. "Last I heard it's still a free country, Sheriff."

Sheriff Harding studied him with a speculative frown. He gave a slight shake of his head and wearily exhaled. "We got off on the wrong foot. My fault. Let's sit down and talk."

The deputy turned sharply to glare at the sheriff as if he'd just committed treason.

"Here?" Mitch asked, his gaze skimming the attentive pool players.

"How about over there in the corner?"

Mitch glanced at the empty table. Only two others were occupied but they were closer to the bar. "Okay."

Curious, Kate followed them, and when the sheriff gave her a questioning look she shrugged and said, "We were about to have dinner."

A ghost of a smile tugged at one side of Mitch's mouth, but he didn't object.

The four of them sat around the small table, the deputy showing his disapproval by jerking his chair out and scraping the wood plank floor. Everyone ignored him except Marjorie, who gave the deputy a dirty look when she showed up to see if they wanted anything.

They ordered iced teas, mostly to be polite, Kate suspected, at least that was her reason. She was just plain nosy and had no intention of leaving until she found out what was going on between the sheriff and Mitch. And why did the deputy look as if he'd like to draw his gun and show Mitch out of town?

As soon as Marjorie left, Sheriff Harding sighed and leveled Mitch with a look he would give a recalcitrant child. Kate knew. She often used the same expression when teaching.

"I know I was touchy earlier," the sheriff began. "Same as a lot of folks around here. There's been some finger-pointing and tempers flaring, and we've just started to get people calmed down. I'm sure you can understand that."

Mitch nodded, but the stubborn set of his jaw hadn't changed. He was on the defensive, and Kate wished she knew why.

"So if you start asking questions, some folks might take it the wrong way. They might even see it as an accusation and get riled up again." The sheriff paused and seemed to study Mitch's face. The remote look in his eyes revealed nothing. "Are you catching my meaning?"

Not quick to respond, Mitch finally said, "I've known most of these folks my whole life. If I was making an accusation, they'd know it."

"I'm sick of this pussyfooting around." The deputy pounded the table with his fist. "The sheriff here is being too polite. We know all about you, Colter."

"Andy," the sheriff drawled out his warning.

"Yeah?" Mitch cocked an eyebrow in amusement. "What's that?"

"You think you're some big hotshot just because you fly planes and used to teach martial arts and work as a personal trainer for prissy Hollywood stars."

Marjorie showed up with their iced teas, and everyone stayed quiet as she moved the glasses from her tray to the table. Then she glanced at the deputy. "And he worked as a bodyguard for that TV actress. Everybody already knows that, Andy. Quit making a damn fool of yourself," she said, huffing as she left the table.

The deputy threw her a sour look, and then brought his attention back to Mitch. "But how many people know you married the woman and it only lasted two months? What happened? Still felt like a hired hand?"

Kate stared at Mitch in disbelief. He'd been married? His parents had said nothing.

He stared impassively at the deputy, but clearly a nerve had been struck. Kate knew Mitch too well not to see the fire in his gray eyes. Or the way that muscle in his jaw flexed when he was holding back.

"Shut up, Barns. This isn't personal." The sheriff made a slashing motion with his hand that said he'd had enough. "The thing is, Colter, this is local business, and we don't like outsiders—"

"Excuse me, Sheriff." Kate couldn't keep silent any longer. "I understand you're fairly new to these parts, so you probably don't realize that the Colter family has been around as long as mine and the Livingstons and Thompsons and several others, the only difference being, the rest of us didn't lose our herd and our livelihood. So I sincerely hope you are not suggesting that Mitch is an outsider."

Sheriff Harding's expression tightened and a dull red crept up his thick neck. "There are some matters regarding the case that you don't understand, Ms. Manning."

"Forgive me." She smiled contritely. "Perhaps it would make you feel better if my brothers or I ask the questions that you think our neighbors would find so disturbing. I assure you, they would suspect no ulterior motives behind our concern."

The man didn't look happy. In fact, he probably wanted to wring her neck for interfering. But she knew he wouldn't dare openly challenge her. Mitch, on the other had, looked highly amused, although he did an admirable job of keeping a straight face.

"I'm famished," she said, and looked around the table. "Anything else?"

Both the sheriff and deputy averted their gazes.

"You having anything, Mitch?" she asked sweetly.

He slowly shook his head, no longer trying to conceal his smile as he reached into his pocket and threw down a twenty.

"Good." She stood, and looked down her nose at the deputy. "Oh, and Andy, you're a jerk."

MITCH FOLLOWED HER OUTSIDE, totally blown away by this assertive side of Kate. He'd always known she had spunk as a kid, but it had been a shy, quiet kind of strength. Not that he couldn't have handled the sheriff and his two-bit sidekick. In fact, had anyone else presumed to undermine his ability to defuse the situation, he would've been pissed. He wouldn't even have allowed it.

As soon as they were on the sidewalk, she spun to face him, her green eyes sparkling, her cheeks pink. Then her gaze darted to the windows. The blinds were open and although it was difficult to see inside past the tinted glass, they both knew it wasn't hard to look out.

"Walk me to my car, will you?" She slid an arm through his, and steered him right before he could clue her in to the fact that he had no intention of letting her drive home. "I know I shouldn't have jumped in," she said quickly. "I apologize."

"No need. I enjoyed the show."

She sighed. "I honestly don't know what's wrong with Sheriff Harding. He's always seemed to be fair and sensible. His deputy is, well, there's no explaining how he got hired. But what's up between you and the sheriff?"

"I called him last week about the status of the rustling investigation and he gave me the runaround. That was the main reason I decided to come in person. But when I talked to him earlier today, he was just as uptight."

She pursed her lips as if she were dying to say something, but was holding back.

"No. I did not imply he wasn't doing his job. I merely wanted a status report on the investigation."

She stopped in front of a small silver SUV and lifted her chin. "I never said you'd do such a thing."

Maybe he'd misread her. Maybe she wanted to know about his brief marriage. Damn. "Is this yours?"

She nodded. "It's a hybrid. I get thirty-four miles to the gallon."

The comment came out of nowhere and made Mitch laugh. "That's very responsible of you."

"Oh, God, you sound like Dennis." She yanked her keys out of her purse. "I'm turning the darn thing in tomorrow and buying a sports car."

"Kate."

"I mean it."

"I'm sure you do." He curled his hand around hers. "But you're not driving."

"I'm perfectly fine to drive. I wouldn't do so otherwise."

He took her by the shoulders and drew her closer, out of hearing distance from the person who'd walked out of the drugstore. "How many shots did you have?"

Her green eyes widened with shock as she regarded him. "You can't do this in the middle of Main Street."

"Do what?"

She moistened her lips, her gaze drifting to his mouth before she looked away. "I thought…" She hunched her shoulders, and he released her. "I have to go. Joe and Clint will be worried."

"Ride home with me, and we'll deal with your car tomorrow," he said, and again saw the defiant lift of her chin. "You probably are fine. Better to play if safe."

She issued a short humorless laugh. "That's me. Dependable, sensible Kate. Always playing it safe. Would you expect anything less? I mean look how far it's gotten me. My life is perfect."

It wasn't just the booze talking, but grief and anger over her life being turned upside down. He hoped he hadn't messed her up more last night. "Put it this way, you just called the deputy a jerk. My guess is he'd love to have a reason to pull you over."

Her expression sobered quickly. "You have a point."

He smiled. "Come on. My old truck isn't riding so hot but it'll get you back to the Sugarloaf. I can bring Clint or Joe back for your car."

"I'd rather they didn't know about, well, any of this."

Mitch started them toward his truck. Obviously she'd forgotten there'd been a couple of Sugarloaf ranch hands playing pool at the next table. "All right, I can bring you back in the morning if that's what you want."

"If it's not too much trouble." She looked miserable.

"What if your brothers did know?"

She blinked at him. "Know I had enough to drink that I had to leave my car in town?"

He shrugged. "Yeah."

"They'd wonder what had gotten into me."

"Right."

"And naturally they'd worry."

"Okay," he drawled out the word, watching the wariness cloud her eyes. "Is that the worst that could happen?"

"I'd have to explain about calling off the wedding, something I planned to do tomorrow, anyway. And which—" she held up a finger "—is no excuse."

"Excuse for what?"

"Drinking too much." She made a face when she realized her admission. "I meant to say, drinking, period."

Grinning, Mitch dug into his pocket for his keys. "This is it."

Kate stared at the old Ford pickup. "Isn't this the same truck you had in high school?"

"Yep, Dad kept it lubed and running for me." He opened the passenger door and waited for her to get in.

She was inspecting the cracked dashboard when he climbed behind the wheel. "It was already old back when you were in school."

He turned the key. "I prefer the term *classic.*"

"Right." She shifted, as if she were trying to get comfortable. "Fix this spring that's poking my fanny and just maybe I'll concede that's it's a classic."

Mitch burst out laughing. "I forgot about that."

"Sure, you're in the driver's seat."

"Slide closer to me, and I'll tell you a secret about that spring."

"What a line."

Mitch pulled away from the curb. "Suit yourself, but I don't want to hear about your bruised rear end tomorrow."

"I promise never to discuss my rear end with you." She scooted to the middle of the bench seat. "Tell me about the spring."

"It was your brother's idea to bust it. I had just gotten my driver's license, and my dad surprised me with the truck. It had been my grandfather's."

"He broke the spring on purpose?"

"Yep."

"Why?"

"So that my dates would have to sit next to me."

She grinned. "You're kidding."

"I'm not."

"That's pretty ridiculous, even for Clint."

"It was Joe."

She whipped her head around to face him. "Not Joe."

"We were barely sixteen. It was pretty funny." Mitch shrugged, but her defensive reaction had caught him off guard.

She vehemently shook her head. "Joe would never do anything so silly. You're confusing him with Clint."

"You'd be surprised," he said calmly, aware that this was an image of her brother that she couldn't grasp. She'd been a child when her parents died and Joe had stepped into the role of patriarch. "Your brother was a kid once, too."

She slumped in her seat, looking tired and sad suddenly. "I don't remember him as a boy. I only remember resenting him for bossing me around so much."

"He was determined to keep you and Clint together on the ranch."

"I know. He gave up college. He gave up so much for us."

"Hey, don't look so blue." He slid a comforting arm around her shoulders. "If the situation were reversed, you or Clint would have done the same."

Sighing, she snuggled closer. "Dependable, steadfast. The Manning curse." She shifted again so that her thigh pressed against his. "By the way, the busted spring plan works."

"Turned out to be genius." He saw now that putting his arm around her might not have been the best idea. Her clean, feminine scent curled inside him, and he was far too aware of the side of her breast brushing his chest.

The smart thing to do would be to take his arm back, put his hands on the wheel and just get her home safe. Instead, he pulled her closer, the sensation of her body against his reawakening all the baser urges that he'd quelled the night before.

What was it with him? There was every reason in the world not to want Kate, especially now when she was reeling from her breakup with Dennis. The last thing she needed was a guy she couldn't count on, who thought only of himself. Just holding her was proof of what an ass he could be.

She moved again, and this time she whimpered softly, a sound that went straight to his cock. Mitch pulled his arm back and shifted away from her, at least a little.

Kate turned her head, her warm sweet breath bathing his jaw. "Mitch?"

"Yeah." He kept his eyes on the road, tightened his hold.

"Were you really married?"

7

THE MINUTE SHE ASKED the question, Kate knew the timing was wrong. His body tensed, his fists visibly tightening on the wheel. She should have waited for him to offer the information, but she'd been so shocked by the deputy's declaration, even more shocked that Mitch hadn't immediately denied the allegation. Which meant it had to be true.

"I'm sorry. I shouldn't pry," she said, only after it appeared he didn't plan on opening the topic for conversation.

"It was brief, stupid and a long time ago. Not much else to tell."

She nibbled her lower lip to keep from bursting with more questions. He hadn't given her nearly enough details, but dare she push for more? "Did your parents know?"

"Not until after the annulment."

Her ears perked up. Annulment? Not a divorce? Not that it mattered. The whole idea of Mitch married, even for a day, was absurdly disconcerting. And childish. Definitely childish. One would think she still had a crush on Mitch.

She wondered how much more rope he'd give her. As

far as she knew he'd worked security for two different actresses, both young, beautiful and blond. "Mandy Pearl, right?"

He threw her an annoyed look. "What difference does it make?"

"Just curious."

He grudgingly nodded. "Just so you know, this isn't for public knowledge."

"Of course," she said indignantly, and then thought for a moment. "Was the wedding ever publicized? I don't read tabloids, but anything to do with Mandy would be newsworthy."

"It was kept under wraps. We were lucky. I was her bodyguard, so no one questioned why I was with her in Vegas that weekend."

"You did *not* get married in one of those cheesy wedding chapels."

"Come on, Kate, I think we've exhausted this subject."

"But—"

His warning look told her to back off, and she wasn't sure why she wanted to know more. It was just such an intriguing notion. Her Mitch married to someone so incredibly famous? Her Mitch *married?*

"One more question and then I promise to shut up."

He abruptly turned the wheel, and pulled the truck off to the shoulder.

Unprepared, Kate slid across the seat and got poked by the spring. "Ouch."

"I have a question. Why does Sheriff Harding feel so threatened he had to dig that deep into my past?" Mitch roughly shoved a hand through his hair, his gaze narrowed at something off in the distance. "I mean, I get the good cop, bad cop thing, but coming at me like that was just plain strange."

At first she thought he was trying to change the subject, but she quickly got that he was genuinely troubled. He also had a point. "Andy was the one who brought all that up."

Mitch turned to look at her as if he'd forgotten she was there. "He doesn't strike me as being very bright. Harding has to be pulling the strings."

She shrugged helplessly. "I met him for the first time last year when I came home for the summer. I saw him once again at Christmas and then last month when I got back here after school let out. I personally don't know much about the sheriff. But if people didn't like him, I would've heard about it." A horrific thought occurred to her. "You're not thinking he's involved in the rustling."

"I don't know what I'm thinking," he said crossly. "He got me all riled just like he wanted."

"At least he doesn't know that. You were as cool as the proverbial cucumber."

He stretched his arm along the back of the seat and studied her. "And you were awesome."

"Me?"

"Jumping to my defense like you did." He picked up a lock of her hair and twirled it around his finger, staring so intently it made her pulse leap. "Why did you cut it?"

Kate silently cleared her throat. "I hated how wild and curly it got."

"I liked it."

"You noticed?"

"After you left the pigtail stage." He smiled when she

made a face. "You used to ride Shiloh down by the stream, and that breeze would come down the canyon, and your hair would be all over the place."

"When did you see me down there?"

"I think it might have been spring break for you, and I'd come to see the folks."

"It was my sophomore year in college." Kate remembered, because that was the last time she'd seen him. Their paths hadn't crossed again until last night. "I didn't see you out there. Why didn't you flag me down?"

"I heard that you'd been having a hard time being away from your brothers and the ranch." He shrugged. "You looked so happy out there, I wanted to give you some space."

Warmth flooded her chest. She didn't know if it was his low soothing voice, or the tender look in his eyes, or the way he played with her hair that lulled her into a peaceful calm she hadn't felt in a long time. "You came and went so quickly that weekend I hardly saw you."

"I would have made a special effort had I known you wanted to."

"Are you just being irritatingly nice because I'm a basket case?"

His eyebrows went up. "I figured you had a lot to pack into that one week and the last thing you wanted was your brothers' friend eating up your time. Bet you had a date every night."

"Right."

"No?"

She rolled her eyes, and leaned back into the protruding spring. She arched her back, and with a start, noticed Mitch's gaze on her jutting breasts.

He lifted his gaze. "You're sitting on that busted spring again."

"I'm painfully aware of that, and I'm gonna smack Joe."

He released her hair, put his hands back on the wheel and jammed the truck in gear. "Move over here and I'll try to get you home before you're completely bruised."

His actions were so abrupt she felt as if she'd said something wrong. She tentatively moved to the middle of the seat and lightly touched his arm. He seemed reluctant to look at her.

"Mitch? What did I do?"

"It's me," he said, looking straight ahead, but not making a move to get on the highway. "Not you."

"At least I know you're not breaking up with me," she said drily.

He turned to her with a puzzled frown. "What?"

"A guy always says that when he wants to let a woman down easily."

Guilt flickered in his eyes before he looked away. So he had used the line before. What guy hadn't? "Take this one at face value."

"This isn't fair. How can I not think this sudden change in you has something to do with me? I'm not drunk, you know. And I have known you all my life. I was just curious, that's all. I didn't mean to wander into forbidden territory."

His jaw tightened, and his hand went back to the gearshift. "I wanted to kiss you, Katie. Damn it, I almost did. Happy?"

Apparently, he'd forgotten they were already in gear and jerked the stick, making that awful grinding sound.

"Don't you dare pull onto the road now." Her heart somersaulted. "Not after admitting that."

"I'm out of line," he said through clenched teeth.

"Because of Dennis?"

He grimaced. "That, too."

She quickly replayed the conversation that seemed to turn the tide. She'd mentioned her brother, then Mitch had called her Katie, and now she understood. "You are such a dope."

Finally, reluctantly, he looked at her. "I'm taking you home now."

"How long do you think you can get away with pretending I'm still a kid?"

"It's more complicated than that. We have history. Our families have history. Your brothers and I are friends, but most importantly, I'm not looking for a relationship."

"Just casual sex?"

"Hell, Katie." He scrubbed at his face. "It's not like that."

"What makes you think sex isn't all I want?"

He slowly shook his head, his mouth pulled into a grim line. "I'm not having this conversation with you."

"Okay, fine." She folded her arms under her breasts, careful not to touch him. "Drive."

"So now you're mad."

"Nope." Sad, and a bit embarrassed that he felt compelled to treat her so kindly, but she wasn't mad. Mitch had always been the kind of guy who every girl in school prayed would take her to the senior prom. Hell, now she knew he'd even been married to one of the most gorgeous women in Hollywood.

He hesitated, and then steered them onto the highway. After a couple of miles, he said, "You're giving me the silent treatment, yet you don't want me to think of you as a kid anymore."

"I'm tired of being manipulated," she said flatly, and stared out the passenger window at the endless acres of yellowed grass and the occasional clump of cacti. She missed spring when the landscape was green and the profusion of purple and pink wildflowers stole your breath away.

"How am I manipulating you?"

"I know you mean well, and that's the only reason I'm not angry. But I don't need to be flattered or coddled or patted on the head."

He looked at her as if she'd slapped him. "Did it ever occur to you that I might just be trying to be a friend? To respect your position, and mine?"

That hurt, but it still wasn't the point. "Real respect means telling the truth. Not deciding what I am or am not capable of hearing. I'm a grown woman, Mitch. By trying to protect me, you're taking away my choices.

The vehicle swerved a bit and he eased off the speed. "So you want me to kiss you?"

"I want the decision to be mine."

He sighed as his hands once again tightened on the wheel. "I have to give that some thought."

"What does that mean?"

"Just what I said. Now, can we drop this? At least for now?"

She lowered her hands to her thighs as she forced herself to be rational and consider things from his angle. He'd confessed something awfully major. He wanted to kiss her. He'd been away for years, and he must still think of her as he'd known her back in the day—just as she kept seeing him as her childhood crush. Maybe they both needed to think this through. "Drive now," she said. "Think later."

WHEN MITCH ARRIVED at the Sugarloaf the next morning, Clint was stacking bales of hay onto the back of an old white pickup. Joe was working in the office, and Kate was somewhere in the house. She still had to pick up her car in town, and he figured he'd be the one to take her if she still hadn't said anything to her brothers.

He pulled on a pair of work gloves that were lying on the ledge of the barn window and went to work helping Clint as he filled him in on his visit to the sheriff. He didn't even leave out the crap the deputy had dug up on him because the tidbit was too juicy for the town gossips to ignore. He figured the five-year secret had about a twenty-four-hour shelf life.

Clint used the back of his wrist to wipe his forehead, and then narrowed his eyes on Mitch. "You son of a bitch. You were married to *the* Mandy Pearl?"

"Yeah, for like ten minutes, and it wasn't all it was cracked up to be." Mitch swung a bale onto the truck. "Something is off with that sheriff. The guy's overreacting. It's not just me. Kate agrees."

Clint frowned. "Kate?"

Mitch hadn't meant to let that slip. "She was at Barney's returning something to Marjorie."

"I was wondering where she was yesterday." He stopped working to drink from a jug of water and stared thoughtfully into the distance. "It does seem odd that he would go to the trouble of doing a background check on you. He obviously feels threatened."

"For no reason. I was nothing but polite and friendly."

Clint passed him the jug. "He's up for reelection next year. The rustling seems to have stopped but no arrests were made. Not to say that folks are tossing blame, but if I were him, I'd be sweating it."

"Then you'd think he would accept all the help he can get." Kate's approach had been silent, and both men turned toward her. "From the little I heard, I assume you're talking about the sheriff."

She was about ten feet away, dressed in white shorts and a stretchy blue top. Mitch had to pull his gaze away from her legs. They looked long enough in jeans, but bare and shapely from midthighs down, they easily ruled his attention.

He met her eyes and nodded. "Morning, Kate."

"Good morning." She smiled at them both and then said to Clint, "I was there yesterday when the sheriff came into Barney's. Andy was with him and he was spoiling for a fight, all right."

Clint frowned at Mitch. "So it was Andy, not the sheriff who gave you a problem."

"Let's say Harding was better at containing himself."

Kate grinned and elbowed Mitch in the ribs, which he took with a surprised grunt. "He's just jealous. A tall, good-looking hunk like you shows up and…" She shrugged. "Between you and Clint in the same town, the poor guy doesn't have a chance on a Saturday night."

Clint snorted, giving his sister a long-suffering look of exasperation.

"Did you eat breakfast this morning?" she asked, switching her attention to him.

"I was late so I grabbed a muffin with my coffee."

"Well, there's leftover pancake batter if you boys are interested." She glanced at Mitch. "There's also some sausage Joe left warming."

"Thanks, I'm good." So this was how she was gonna play it. She'd clearly done some thinking about what had happened in the truck and decided to treat him like one of her brothers. Good. Better for both of them. He'd decided pretty much the same thing, after his cold shower.

She placed her hands on her hips, making her top stretch tautly over her breasts. "What are you going to do now?"

He kept his expression neutral. "Finish helping your brother load this truck."

"I meant about the rustling."

"Only one thing I can do," he said, and picked up another bale. He couldn't stand there facing her. Not with her nipples prodding the stretchy material of her blouse. He had to remember to keep a pair of sunglasses in his pocket.

"How soon will you be leaving?" She sounded a bit relieved.

"Leave? I haven't found out anything yet."

"If the sheriff isn't going to cooperate, what else can you do?" She stared at him with a puzzled look.

Clint pulled off a glove, his gaze trained on the driveway as a big dark sedan turned off the dirt road. "You recognize that car, Kate? Looks familiar."

She turned around and shaded her eyes. "I've seen it in town, but I don't know who owns it."

Mitch could've sworn she had freckles on her legs as a kid.

She didn't now. In fact, the color was a light golden tone, not sunbaked, but still on the creamy side. The night before last had been dark, and he'd been too stunned to notice every detail. Nothing missed his notice now, especially not the tempting swell of her backside.

"I think I know who it is." Clint pulled off his other glove. "That Realtor who sold the Baxters' place."

Wary suddenly, Mitch paid closer attention to the car as it headed toward them. A Realtor had contacted his father a couple of days after they'd left the ranch. The idea that his parents had thought about selling had spurred Mitch into action.

The man parked near the barn, and then climbed out of his late model car. Average height, late thirties, he wore a light blue Western-cut suit, a tan Stetson and spanking-new cowboy boots. Had to be from Houston or Dallas. One of those weekend cowboys was Mitch's guess.

"Howdy," he said, removing his hat and nodding at Kate as he approached. "Name's Levi Dodd." He extended his hand to Clint, while Mitch removed his gloves. "I hope y'all don't mind my dropping by unannounced."

"No problem." Clint made the introductions all around. "What can we do for you?"

"I heard Mr. Colter was a good friend of yours," he said, then turning to Mitch, "I stopped by your folks' place first, and when you weren't there, I was hoping to find you here."

Mitch tensed. If Clint was right and this guy was a Realtor, Mitch didn't have a damn thing to say to him, not when it came to the ranch. "You found me."

The man seemed pleasant enough with his country boy demeanor and toothy grin, but when he took a business card from his breast pocket and handed it over, Mitch needed only to see the word *Realtor* for his defenses to rise.

He studied the card for a second, and then passed it back to the man. "Can't imagine what I can do for you, Mr. Dodd."

"Please, call me Levi." His heavy dark brows dipping in a bewildered frown, he gestured for Mitch to keep the card. "I assumed your mama or daddy would've mentioned me."

Mitch shrugged and stuck the card in the back pocket of his jeans. "If they did, I don't recall."

"Would anyone like some iced tea or lemonade?" Kate asked, her voice an octave higher than usual.

"None for me, thanks," Mitch said, pointedly pulling on the work gloves and eyeing the stack of bales that needed to be moved.

"No, thank you, ma'am," Levi said. "Mr. Colter, might we have a word in private?"

After an awkward silence, Clint said, "I think I will have some of that lemonade, Kate." He tossed his gloves onto the bed of the pickup. "I'll go back to the house with you."

"Wait." Mitch held up a hand. "Mr. Dodd, you're in the business of buying and selling, right?"

The man nodded warily.

"Since my family is doing neither, I don't see what we have to discuss."

An annoyed flush crawled up the Realtor's face. His smile seemed forced. "I talked to your father a couple of weeks ago, and he told me they were seriously thinking of putting both the house and the land on the market."

"That hasn't been decided yet."

Dodd's head reared back in open surprise. "You aren't thinking about listing with another agent, are you? Because I assure you—"

"Nope."

"If you're worried about getting a fair price, I suggest you talk to the Baxters. They'll verify that I got them top dollar for their—"

"Look, Mr. Dodd, this is nothing personal." Damn right this was personal. That was Colter land. Had been for over a hundred years. The thought of anyone else living in the old brick house made Mitch's stomach turn. He caught Kate's curious look, and suddenly wished he had taken the man aside. But he'd let his temper get the better of him. "I doubt we'll be needing the services of a Realtor."

The man stared back, a dumbfounded expression on his face.

"But the place is sitting vacant. What good is it doing you?"

"Vacant?" Mitch met the man's eyes with unwavering persistence. "I'm there."

"But for how long? I could have it listed and ready to show as soon as you leave."

Mitch smiled. "What makes you think I'm leaving?" Out of the corner of his eye, he saw Kate sag against the oak hitching post. He stopped thinking about real estate and wondered why she wanted him to leave so badly. It had to be because of his confession yesterday. She'd done some thinking, all right, and figured out that kissing him was worse than taking back that fool Dennis.

8

HUMIDITY WAS HIGH, but not nearly as thick as the tension shrouding the air around them. Kate clasped her hands tightly together, her gaze glued to Mitch. Was he serious about hanging around, or was he just trying to get rid of the guy? She couldn't tell. She glanced at Clint to gauge his reaction, but he'd always had a great poker face.

She took a deep breath, her thoughts splintering in several directions. Had she only assumed that Mitch'd be here for a few days? Had he specifically mentioned a time frame? No, she was safe. Mitch had a job, a busy life in Florida. He had no intention of sticking around.

She had to believe that. All she'd been able to think about last night had been his admission. And what might happen next. Only, she hadn't been able to get past the fact that Mitch Colter wanted to kiss her. She'd hoped that his leaving soon would take the questions off the table.

With a glum expression, Mr. Dodd said, "I made a long drive out here because your father gave me the impression that y'all were interested in selling."

Mitch shrugged. "A phone call would've saved you the trip."

The Realtor snorted. "You've got me there, partner."

He scanned the barn and bunkhouse, and then squinted toward the corrals and back pastures. "Y'all got a nice spread here. Don't suppose you'd be interested in selling a piece of it."

Kate sputtered, unable to articulate her outrage at the thought. Clint's eyes gleamed with menace. Was the man out of his mind?

Mr. Dodd quickly got the message. He threw up his hands in defeat. "Figured I'd ask. Can't blame a guy for trying to make a living." He looked as if he were dying to say something more, but wisely kept his mouth shut. Instead, he withdrew a white linen handkerchief from his pocket and blotted his face, and then offered a hand to Mitch. "You've got my card if you change your mind. If I come by this way next week, I may swing by and give you a shout."

Kate watched with interest as renewed tension seemed to saturate Mitch's body. He graciously accepted Mr. Dodd's handshake, but if the man had a lick of sense he'd see that Mitch would not be happy with him showing up again. She totally understood. The idea of anyone besides a Manning owning their land chilled her to the bone. Still, Mitch had never exhibited that kind of attachment to the land.

The three of them silently watched the Realtor coast down the driveway toward the road. That he was even eyeing their land as he drove filled her with indignation, and triggered a similar response in Clint, judging by the scowl on his face.

"Did you know your dad had talked to him?" Clint asked, turning to study Mitch's face.

"He mentioned it," Mitch admitted, his steely gaze

following the dark sedan's exit from the property. "That's why I decided to come."

"I know you hate seeing the place sold, but if your dad doesn't want to work cattle and hire some more help, the ranch might be too much for them."

"I want him to have a choice." The way Mitch yanked on the gloves mirrored his anger. "Those bastards stole more than cattle."

Clint and Kate exchanged worried glances. "You know we'll help you any way we can," Clint said calmly. "Just give us the word."

"There is something you can do. It's no small favor so you'll need to talk it over with Joe."

Kate couldn't keep quiet a second longer. "For heaven's sake, Joe will be on board with anything you need."

The hard look in Mitch's eyes receded as they met hers, and his mouth curved in a warm smile. "Humor me. I'll lay out my plan and the three of you discuss whether you're amenable to it tonight. If the answer is no, so be it. No hard feelings."

Kate arched her brows at him. "Imagine the situation reversed," she said, "Now, how can we help you?"

Mitch's smile broadened. "When did she get to be such a little wildcat?" he asked Clint, his attention still on Kate.

Clint chuckled. "It's been hell since she reached puberty."

She huffed, started to make a wisecrack but then realized her brother was watching them with far too much curiosity. "Do we have to drag it out of you?"

Mitch sobered. "I want to borrow a couple dozen head of cattle. Move them to our north pasture to graze, and then spread it around town that the Colters are back in business."

"As bait," Clint said, nodding thoughtfully. "In case the rustlers are still in the area."

"Yep. They'll find out I'm there alone, figure I'm easy pickings. They're familiar with the layout, and we know they aren't shy about going back for seconds. I'll set up surveillance equipment that I can monitor from the house, and naturally I'll guarantee the cattle. If I screw up and the bastards get them, I'll reimburse you top dollar."

Kate listened in stunned silence. She didn't give a crap about risking the cattle, but what he was talking about doing would take a long time. He could be here for a month. Or longer.

"Hell, Mitch, the cattle are yours and you're not guaranteeing anything. That's downright insulting," Clint said. "I'm confident in speaking for all of us."

Kate almost missed her cue, but then quickly nodded. "You'll need help with surveillance."

"They'll only strike at night. I'll get some shut-eye during the day and stay on the monitors from dark till dawn."

"Man." Grimacing, Clint rubbed the back of his neck. "I wish I could help you there, but the thing is, I might be gone for a couple of weeks. I could send Pete or Silas over—"

"No offense…I know they've both been with you a long time and they're trustworthy, but the fewer people who know about the setup the better."

Kate switched her attention to Clint. He rarely went farther than Dallas or Houston. Although she had a feeling she knew the answer, she asked, "Where are you going?"

He picked up his hat and settled it back on his head, a big grin spreading across his face. "Dory has some vacation time coming, and she's going to show me around Hawaii."

"Who's Dory?" At Clint's smitten expression, one corner of Mitch's mouth quirked up, and he glanced at Kate as if they shared a secret.

The intimacy made her blush. "She was one of my roommates in college who came for the weekend."

"Yeah, you should've gotten here earlier. There were three of them. Knockouts, every one of them." Clint shrugged. "Of course they're all spoken for now, and I got the best one."

"Spoken for?" Mitch threw a playful punch at Clint's shoulder. "My man, tell me that you and Joe haven't bitten the dust."

Like they'd done as kids, Clint clipped him back. "I didn't say that. Didn't you hear? Kate's the one about to take the plunge."

She felt the blood drain from her face, felt Mitch's eyes on her, but she couldn't bring herself to look at him.

"I won't need any help," Mitch said, diverting the conversation. "I'll pick up equipment in Houston and then set up the cameras before I call attention to myself by moving the herd over. If you don't mind, I'm thinking I might inject a few of them with RFID chips."

"Definitely." Clint was all business again. "I've been trying to convince Joe that's the way to go. The Dandridge Ranch and T&H Cattle Company both have jumped on the bandwagon. We're the only large ranch still operating in the dark ages."

The new direction of the conversation quickly pulled

Kate away from her guilt at not telling her brothers the truth. She sympathized with Clint. Joe was stubborn about doing things the way they'd always done them, she knew, although she tried to stay out of their business dealings. "RFID," she repeated. "Radio frequency identification, right?"

Clint and Mitch both nodded, and Mitch added, "The cattle can either be injected or tagged, and then the chip is read by a scanner. The information on the sex, breed, owner, even the sire if you want, is fed into law enforcement databases. Hard to move or sell the stolen cattle after that."

"Exactly. Over at the T&H they even do retinal scans. It's almost like a fingerprint." Clint let out a long breath. "That's why the bigger ranches haven't been hit. Everyone assumes they're operating in the twenty-first century." Lowering his voice, he added, "We have a good crew that's been with us for a long time. They're all skittish about the rustling, and I'm sure they keep their mouths shut about what an easy target we are."

Kate wrapped her arms around herself, feeling a bit shaky. She hated thinking about the rustlers, and had sympathized with her neighbors who'd been victimized, but she hadn't realized that the Sugarloaf was vulnerable.

Clint shook his head with regret. "Rotten timing for me to be taking off for a couple of weeks, and I'd postpone the trip except that's when Dory can get time off. I'll talk to Joe. I bet he'll be willing to give you a hand with surveillance while I'm gone."

"Um, I don't think you can count on Joe," Kate said hesitantly.

Both men looked quizzically at her.

Mitch said, "I don't need help."

Clint asked, "Why?"

"He's meeting Lisa in Tulsa for a few days. I don't know about after."

Clint frowned. "When did he tell you that?"

Kate glanced over her shoulder toward the house. "He didn't. Lisa told me, and I probably shouldn't have said anything, but I wanted to give you a heads-up."

"No wonder he's getting a jump on payroll," Clint said with a slow, knowing nod of his head. "Good for him."

Mitch grunted. "What the hell is going on with you boys?"

"Told ya, you missed out." Clint caught him off guard with a mock jab to the side of his jaw.

Mitch gave him a warning look that was tempered by a tug at the corners of his mouth, and made a mockery of his curling fists.

"I could do it," Kate said quietly.

They both looked at her.

"It's just watching a monitor, right?"

The playfulness vanished from Mitch's face. "What happens if the bait works?"

"Then you'll need an extra rifle, won't you?"

Mitch shook his head, his lips set in a grim line. "No way."

She put a hand on her hip. "I'm a good shot, and you damn well know it."

"Come on, Katie." Mitch glanced at Clint for help. "Target practice is a whole different ball game."

"Don't Katie me. Besides, I won't shoot anyone. Aiming over their heads should get the point across."

"I don't know, Kate," Clint began tentatively. "I mean, helping with surveillance is one thing, but you'd have to promise not to—"

She threw up her hands in warning. "Don't even say it."

Mitch folded his arms across his broad chest, his biceps bulging beneath his black T-shirt sleeves. "Moot point. The answer is no."

She glared at him. "You don't get a vote here."

"Dennis would probably have something to say about this," Clint said.

"Dennis can go—" She cut herself off, took a deep calming breath and lifted her chin. "Don't worry about Dennis. In fact, I have to talk to you and Joe later about a personal matter. In the meantime…" She couldn't look at Mitch. "If you or any of the boys are going into town, I'd appreciate a lift so I can pick up my car."

"Your car?" Clint frowned. "Did it break down?"

Kate started to back toward the house, before her bravado faltered. "I ended up playing pool with some of the guys at Barney's yesterday and had too much to drink," she said with calm defiance. "So I had to get a ride with Mitch. I'll be in the house."

She turned and tried to monitor her pace. If she suddenly ran for cover as she wanted to, it would undo the brave front she'd just put up. It was ridiculous that at twenty-seven she felt she had to explain herself to her brothers. Clint had left his car in town a time or two because he'd been drinking beer with his friends. Though not Joe, he was far too sensible. She wasn't sure she would've been so blasé had Joe been standing there just now. The thought annoyed her, but it was the truth.

She squared her shoulders. This was a good jumping-off point. Things were going to start changing around here. She wasn't a kid anymore, and everyone had better get used to the idea. Including Mitch Colter.

WITH ADMIRATION, MITCH stared after her retreating back. He was proud of her for laying it out there for her brother, letting him know she was in charge of her own life. It was something Mitch needed to get through his own thick skull. But she'd also left him to face a very confused Clint, and Mitch wasn't sure how he was going to answer the slew of questions about to be thrown his way.

"What the hell has gotten into her? Kate never drinks too much. She hardly drinks." Clint took off his hat and used his arm to wipe his forehead. When she disappeared into the house, Clint turned to him. "Why didn't you tell me you had to bring her home?"

Mitch shrugged. "It never came up."

"Were you shooting pool with her?"

"Nope."

"Was her fiancé there?"

Uneasy with the direction of the conversation, Mitch shook his head. "I don't think so." He checked his watch. "I have time to go to Houston and pick up the surveillance equipment today. But I still want you to run my idea by Joe before I do anything."

"It's not a problem," Clint said distractedly. "Who was she playing pool with?"

Mitch hesitated, not wanting to get in the middle. Yet, despite everything, he understood exactly where his friend was coming from. It was hard not to be protective around Kate. She was… Shit. He was such a hypocrite. "There were some Sugarloaf hands there," he answered. "But mostly she was with two new guys from the Double R."

"Not Brad Jackson."

"A guy named Brad was one of them," Mitch said, not liking the pinched look on Clint's face.

He muttered a curse. "What the hell was she doing with that guy?"

"What do you know about him?"

"Not much," Clint admitted. "But he's a cocky son of a bitch. He was here over the weekend, strutting around like a damn rooster."

"Reynolds can't be paying much after getting half his herd wiped out. How did this Brad character and his buddy end up at the Double R?"

"Beats me." Clint's brows drew together. "As much as I don't like the guy I've got no call to think he's dirty, if that's what you're thinking. Don't recall any problems since he hired on."

"Anybody else new around here that you'd consider needs watching?"

Clint sighed. "I honestly don't know." He slapped his hat against his thigh. "I don't like the idea of Brad cozying up to Kate. But if I say anything to her, she'll jump down my throat."

Mitch smiled. "Can't blame her. She is an adult."

"Still naive, though. You said you haven't met her fiancé, right?"

Mitch shook his head, glanced purposely at his watch again, hoping to derail Clint. Man, he'd be glad once Kate filled her brothers in on the broken engagement.

"I'll be interested to hear your take on the guy." He apparently misread Mitch's sudden tension and added,

"Yeah, I know it's none of my business, and I won't say anything more on the subject."

Relieved, Mitch exhaled slowly.

"I have a favor to ask you," Clint said, gazing toward the house. "Keep an eye on Kate while you're here."

Hell, just yesterday he'd vowed he wouldn't let her out of his sight, but being this close to her wasn't easy, either. "I'll do what I can, but I don't know how much I'll be around. Holed up at the ranch mostly. I probably won't have to worry about daylight hours, but I gotta get some sleep sometime."

"That's not a bad idea." Clint thoughtfully reached for the jug of water.

"What?" His gut told Mitch he wasn't going to like this.

"She volunteered to help you. Let her."

"Are you nuts?"

"Don't let her have a rifle. If the time comes and you need backup, she can at least make the call."

Mitch frowned. "Most of the surveillance will be done at night. I'm sure she has better things to do."

"Trust me, she doesn't. She sees Dennis maybe twice a week. It's really kind of weird the way they…" Clint uncapped the jug, briskly shaking his head. "All I'm saying is, if she has time to be hanging out at Barney's, she'd be better off sticking close to you. And that's not to say I suspect Brad or those other newer hands."

Mitch caught his meaning. Out here, to accuse a man of rustling these days was no less serious than a hundred years ago when they'd hang the thief without a trial. "I don't know." Mitch sighed. "I'll talk to her."

"I appreciate it. You still going to Houston?"

"After you talk to Joe."

Clint took a swig of water and then backhanded his mouth. "You're as stubborn as Kate. I'll go tell him now. Take her with you to Houston, then on the way back she can get her car."

Mitch didn't respond. Even if he left now he'd wouldn't be back until after dark, and Kate needed to have a conversation with her brothers.

"I'll take her into town," Mitch said finally, "but I've reconsidered going to Houston today. I think I know where I can get the equipment I need, but I'm gonna make some calls first to make sure I'm not chasing my tail."

"Come to the house with me," Clint said and started in that direction. "If you want I can give the T&H a call. They have a heck of a security setup. Their barns, corrals, stables, pens, even the main house are all monitored."

"Since the rustling started?"

"Nah, Clyde went state of the art as soon as old man Thompson died. They even use helicopters for roundup now. I keep telling Joe...we need to step up our game."

"I agree with you." Mitch knew Joe was stubborn, though he didn't remember him being that pigheaded. But then, as the oldest, he'd taken on a huge responsibility for someone so young. Maybe change frightened him. "It's gonna take a few bucks, so I can't do it overnight, but I plan on modernizing our ranch. I'm licensed to fly a chopper. Maybe someday we can split the cost of a secondhand bird."

Clint stopped and stared at Mitch. "Sounds like you're talking about staying permanently."

"Well, my father will need some help to get up and

running again. I'll have to stick around at least that long." The explanation sounded lame, even to Mitch. He'd been thinking out loud, and the strange thing was he hadn't considered staying for the long term. "That was a thoughtless remark. Forget it, okay?"

"Man, I'd love to see you come back, and that's all I'll say on the subject." Clint turned toward the house and then paused again. "About Kate shooting pool and drinking at Barney's…let's not mention that in front of Joe."

Mitch chuckled. "Why? What is he going to do, ground her?"

Clint's mouth twisted wryly. "He'd sure try."

Mitch walked slowly, letting Clint get ahead, but the man's words lingered. With brothers like Clint and Joe, it was amazing Kate had any gumption, let alone what he'd seen at Barney's. She must have fought long and hard to find the courage to stand up to those two, and here he was trying to rein her in, too.

9

The next day, after Mitch returned from Houston, he went straight to the Sugarloaf. Standing at the front door, he wondered if he shouldn't have gone home to shower and change first. Too late now. He knocked again.

Kate opened the door, wearing an oversized blue T-shirt, her hair pulled back in a sloppy ponytail. Her eyes widened when she saw him, and she self-consciously tucked a wayward lock of hair behind her ear. She seemed a bit out of sorts.

Belatedly, Mitch realized he should've called first. "Is this a bad time?"

"No. Come in." She stepped back, pulling the door wider.

"Are the guys around?"

"Joe should be back soon. Clint's upstairs on the phone with Dory." She glanced over her shoulder. "It's so weird seeing my brothers act like two teenage girls."

Mitch grinned. "Did you tell them that?"

"I tease Clint constantly." She led the way into the family room. "I give Joe a wider berth. This is all very new for him. I'm just glad to see him so happy." She motioned for Mitch to sit on the brown leather couch.

He hesitated. Damn, he wished he'd called first. She

seemed understandably subdued, and he had a feeling that the last thing she wanted to do was entertain him until Clint showed up. "This could've waited until tomorrow."

She faced him with a wan smile. "I'm okay," she said, "really. I told them last night, in case you're wondering. No details. Just that Dennis and I both had second thoughts."

Mitch glanced toward the stairs to be sure they were still alone. "Did you tell them that I know?"

"That would raise too many questions. We'll pretend I just told you." She sighed. "I've always told Joe and Clint everything. But not this. You and my college friends are the only ones who know what happened the other night."

Tentatively he put an arm around her, feeling awkward with the surrogate brother role. Ironic, since that's how he'd always treated her in the past, and that's what she needed from him now. "I know it sounds like a platitude and it's a difficult truth to see when the pain is still new, but the guy really isn't worth it. You deserve better."

She pulled away. "I know. I do. It's not just about Dennis. If I seem a bit off it's about Joe and Clint, and how truly happy I am for them."

"This is your happy look?"

She rolled her eyes at him. "It's just that I keep replaying what you said the other night about Joe being a kid once. He's worked so hard since my parents died. Clint, too. He didn't have to come back after college. Two Dallas companies tried to recruit him in the middle of his senior year. Joe urged him to consider the offers, but he wanted to come back and help run the ranch. In fact, he tried talking Joe into going back to school. Remember? Joe had always wanted to be a veterinarian."

Mitch nodded. "Pete and Silas have been working for your family since before you were born. Don't you think that if Joe really wanted to go back to school he would've made it happen? We both know how, let's say, determined Joe can be."

"I know, but—"

He put a finger to her lips. They were soft and moist, and not something he should've noticed.

"You're sweet." She got up on tiptoes, leaned in and kissed him on the cheek.

He involuntary tensed, unsure of what she'd been about to do. As soon as she moved back, disappointment stabbed at him. Okay, what the hell was that about?

"Did you get the surveillance equipment?" She sat on one end of the couch and curled her legs under her.

"Some of it. I decided the job was too big for me to do quickly enough here by myself, so the rest will be delivered and installed tomorrow morning." He lowered himself onto the opposite end of the overstuffed couch.

"Will it be operational by tomorrow night?"

"Should be. Then I can bring the cattle over the next day."

"I think Clint already talked to Pete about making sure a couple of men are available to help." Her lips parted, and she blinked. "I'm being rude. Want something to drink?"

"Sure. It's been hot today."

"Mind helping yourself?"

"What about you?" he asked as he got to his feet. He knew this house as well as his own. How many afternoons and weekends had he spent here shooting pool or playing darts with Clint and Joe?

"Anything that does not have alcohol in it."

Mitch smiled at the face she made, and then set off for the kitchen. He got himself a beer and Kate an iced tea with exactly half a glass of crushed ice, two wedges of lemon and a sprig of mint. Funny, how he recalled precisely how she liked it.

"Somebody refinished the dining room table and the china hutch," he commented when he returned with their drinks. "They look good."

"Thanks." She accepted her glass of tea, noted the lemon wedges and mint, and smiled. "That was me. A couple of summers ago. I hadn't done anything like it before so I practiced on my vanity table."

"Hey, maybe you can give me some pointers." He shrugged. "If I have some time, I might tackle some of the furniture my parents left and surprise them."

Her brows drew together in a frown. "You think they'll come back?"

"I don't know."

She worried her lower lip, studying him closely, and looking as if she had a hundred more questions. All she said was, "The company who's going to install the cameras, I assume they're coming from Houston."

"Yep, they'll have to come through town but they use a truck with a furniture company logo. They're a top notch security operation. No one will know what they're carrying."

Kate laughed softly. "But of course everyone for a hundred miles will be wondering who's ordered new furniture."

"Some things about small town living I don't miss." He shook his head and then took a pull of beer.

"Some things, huh? Meaning there are things you do miss?"

"Sure," he said with a non-committal shrug.

"Like?"

"Like a certain lady with auburn hair and gorgeous green eyes." His teasing clearly fell flat.

She tensed, and stared down at her hands.

"Kate?"

"You don't have to do that."

"Do what?"

Behind them, the stairs creaked. Had to be Clint. Great timing.

Kate darted a look of dread over her shoulder. In three seconds her face transformed. If Mitch didn't know any better he would've totally believed the smile that she'd miraculously summoned.

"I thought I heard your voice," Clint said, reaching the last step, Mitch knew because it also creaked, and always had. "You get everything done in Houston?"

"Yep. By tomorrow night I should be in business." His gaze went to Kate as she rose from the couch.

"I'm gonna grab a beer. I'll be right there," Clint called out on his way to the kitchen.

She nervously adjusted her ponytail. "I'll leave y'all to discuss moving the cattle."

"Kate, wait."

She hesitated, but refused to look at him. He wanted to know what he'd said to upset her, but she didn't seem as if she were willing to have that discussion. And then there was Clint who was about to return at any minute.

He cleared his throat. "So we're still on for tomorrow, right?"

She turned to frown quizzically at him.

"To help me with surveillance," he said. "I figure we'll take a dry run. Make sure you understand the equipment and we're on the same page before the cattle are in place." She looked suspiciously as if she'd reconsidered her offer, so he added, "I'm counting on you, Kate. Don't let me down."

KATE PARKED AT THE SIDE of the house as Mitch had instructed her to do. The sun had set several minutes ago so it wasn't dark yet but once it was, her car wouldn't be visible from the road or the driveway. Tonight Mitch would show her how to use the monitoring equipment, and tomorrow a couple of the Sugarloaf hands would round up and move the cattle to the Colters' back pasture.

After that, word would spread quickly. By supper, half the people in the county would know that the Colter ranch was back in business, and by breakfast the next morning the other half would have caught up on the news.

She stood at the front door, poised to knock, firmly reminding herself that all she had to do was treat Mitch like one of her brothers. That was the only way they'd get through however many nights they'd be stuck together. If she forced herself to think of him the way she did Clint or Joe, then maybe she wouldn't lie in bed, staring at the ceiling, unable to sleep, wondering what it would be like to kiss him. Really kiss him.

That thought alone was enough to make her stomach tighten. Kissing Mitch had been the stuff of dreams for so much of her life. Wanting to do a lot more than kiss was a relatively recent addition to her repertoire. Which made it imperative that she keep her wits about her, and not let her attraction to him get out of hand.

She wasn't an idiot. She knew she was still reeling from Dennis's betrayal. Which was no time to even think about sex. Even if she believed with all her heart that it was nothing more than scratching that itch, would she be right? Or would she wake up one day and realize she'd used her good friend to make herself feel better? No matter how she sliced it, she had to keep her legs crossed and her thoughts pure.

Just as she was about to knock, her fist still raised in midair, he opened the door. "Hey," Mitch said, and stepped back. His hair was damp, his chin smooth as if he'd just shaved. He smelled clean and deliciously male, and not only did she clench her stomach but she had to press her legs together to stop the thrum. So much for pure thoughts. "Come on in."

"I parked where you told me," she said, feeling nervous suddenly. She'd purposely left her hair in the messy ponytail she favored when she wasn't going anywhere, and she'd kept her makeup to a minimum. After all, she didn't get made up for Clint or Joe.

"Good." He closed the door and then led her to the stairs. "You want something before we go up?"

"Maybe later." Her gaze followed the cherry banister to the second floor. "Is that where you installed the monitors?"

"Better up there in case company stops by." He studied her for a moment, and then started up the stairs.

She held back just far enough to get a good view of his backside. His jeans were worn and snug fitting, and even though she'd always thought he had a spectacular body with those lean hips and broad shoulders, she hadn't fully appreciated what a fine ass he had.

"I'm using Susie's old room," he said, "since it faces the pasture. I brought out her dresser and pushed the rest of the furniture to the back wall but it's still cramped in there."

Kate pulled herself out of her preoccupation and followed him down the hall. "I think her kids used that room when they'd come to visit your parents. I didn't get to see Haley and Taylor the last couple times they were here. They must almost be teenagers by now."

"They're both in high school."

"Wow, already? Susie's only four years older than you, right?"

"Thank you for reminding me."

Kate laughed. "I'm surprised your parents aren't giving you a hard time about not producing your share of grandchildren."

"Believe me, they have plenty to say on the subject." He stopped to let her enter first, but left her little room. "However, they do expect me to get married first so there is that small problem."

She squeezed by him, her pulse speeding up when her fanny rubbed him in a most strategic spot. Not her fault. He could've given her more room. "Do you ever think about getting married, or having kids?"

Groaning, he muttered, "Oh, man, this is gonna be a long night."

"Well, excuse me for trying to make conversation." She folded her arms and faced one of three monitors that were lined up near the window. The curtains were parted, and she could see in the distance the now-empty pasture where the Colters' herd once grazed. It was sad to think of how much had changed for everyone in their close community, starting with her parents' untimely death.

"You forgot. I tried getting married once. It didn't work."

She turned around, surprised he brought up the subject. "Didn't sound like it was a real marriage, though."

"It wasn't." He rolled an office chair to the middle monitor. "Sit down and tell me if this is comfortable."

She did as he asked, shifting, unable to find an acceptable position. She leaned over looking for a lever to adjust the seat.

"What are you doing?"

"It needs to be lower."

He crouched beside her, and fidgeted under the seat. The bottom lowered with a sudden thump, startling her. She clutched his shoulder. "Is that better?" he asked, looking up at her.

How could she not have noticed how long his lashes were? Enviably long. Dark and thick and totally unfair. He even had defined lower lashes. That was just wrong.

"Why don't you look at the monitor?" he suggested. "Tell me if it's the right height."

Humiliation seared its way up her neck and filled her cheeks. "I was noticing your lashes," she murmured as she stared hard at the monitor and gingerly released his shoulder. "This is fine."

"My eyelashes?"

She wished he'd get up. Hunkered down like that he was too close. As it was, her sensitive palm stubbornly held on to the memory of his muscled shoulder. She cleared her throat. "I think I will get something to drink before we get started."

"This is a bad idea, isn't it?" he said, without moving, his gaze too focused on her face.

"What?"

"Come on, Kate." He grasped both arms of her chair and leaned toward her. His warm minty breath touched her chin, bathed the side of her jaw.

She tensed, her nerves quivering, waiting to see what he would do next. And then she realized he was using the arms for support to push himself to his feet. He straightened to his full height, moved back and offered her a hand.

Ignoring it, she got up on her own. "I should've brought some tea. You probably don't have any."

"I do. Lemon and mint, too."

"Oh. Thanks." She made sure they didn't touch as she maneuvered past him. Why did he think this wasn't a good idea?

Was he worried she had designs on him? The thought irritated her.

Okay, so she might have made a fool of herself the night she'd caught Dennis with that woman. But those were extenuating circumstances, and after the evening at Barney's, hadn't she gone out of her way to treat Mitch no differently than she did her brothers?

They had to clear the air if they wanted to work together. Once she told him she wasn't about to change their relationship in any way, she'd lock herself in a corner. Over the next few nights she'd relax, figure out what she was going to do about her future, help a family friend, and nothing more. Surely two grown adults could put physical attraction in its proper perspective. They had to. Otherwise, her nerves would be shot inside of a week. This was on her. She had to initiate the conversation. She stopped, braced herself and then turned back to him.

He was right behind her, a scant breath away.

Their eyes met and the ground shifted. She was supposed to do something now, right? Say something? She just couldn't remember what.

10

MITCH TOLD HIMSELF there was no other way to handle the persistent tension between them. They had to be certain they could work together without distraction. Tonight was the time to find out if that was possible. By tomorrow, once the cattle were in place, there would be too much at stake.

He touched the corner of her mouth with his thumb, searched her expectant green eyes and inhaled the warm sweetness of her skin. Unruly tendrils of hair curled around her face, offering him a glimpse of the old Kate. But only a glimpse. When he pictured her now in his mind's eye, she was this woman. Whom he wanted as he'd wanted little else.

He saw the same fire in her gaze, and he bent his head only to stop short as she placed her hands on his chest. She leaned into him. Whispered, "Hold me, just for a moment."

Her earnest request startled him. Is that all she wanted? Simple human contact, a comforting arm around her? Damn it to hell, she'd given him the signals yesterday, but had he caught on? This conversation was clearly one-sided, and he'd better get that through his thick skull.

He wrapped his arms around her, holding her close

and lightly brushed his lips on top of her head. Her body seemed to shrink into itself, and he silently cursed the thoughtless kiss he'd been about to impose on her. She was still hurting, and all she wanted was the comfort and reassurance she feared asking of her brothers.

Her heartfelt sigh was nearly his undoing. "Thank you," she said.

"What for?"

"For not letting me make a total fool of myself the other night. For not letting me do something I'd regret. For being my friend."

Mitch briefly closed his eyes. He was such an ass. For two nights he'd lain awake, obsessing over how tempting she'd looked lying in his bed. Hell, it wasn't as if he'd been deprived of sex, so what was his problem?

"Mitch?" She stirred in his arms until he loosened his hold. "I know I've messed things up between us, but I swear, my only goal in being here is to help you catch those rustlers." She moved back until he took his hands from her. "Who knows? They may have moved on as everyone seems to think, and you won't have to worry anymore."

"Not good enough. I want to catch them."

"I mean, I don't want to see them hurt anyone else of course, but I'll be glad if the people around here can start resting easy."

"You're more charitable than I am. I want to see them prosecuted as well as make restitution to everyone they stole from. But only after I have them alone for about fifteen minutes."

Kate pursed her lips. "I understand. I wouldn't mind taking a few licks at them myself."

He smiled. "I'd hold them down for you."

"I won't need your help," she said, straightening and pulling her shoulders back.

He tried not to look at her breasts, but standing in that position, the way they filled out her T-shirt. "You want to go down to the kitchen with me, or shall I bring the tea upstairs?"

"I'll go with you."

"Great."

She frowned at him. "Such overwhelming enthusiasm."

"Look, I cleaned up some, but the place has been vacant awhile."

"Don't worry about it. I can help spruce things up."

"I wanted to hire someone from town to do the housekeeping, but it's better that no one sees the surveillance equipment."

"We can handle it. What else will we have to do while we're sitting around waiting for the bad guys to make a move?"

That's exactly what he was worried about.

THE NEXT EVENING KATE arrived early with a basket full of biscuits and chicken and salad makings for their dinner. She also brought an overnight bag with clothes and toiletries, which she kept in the car. Mitch hadn't suggested she spend the night, but as Clint had pointed out, it made sense. Even if she took the first shift watching the monitors, it meant she'd be driving home in the early-morning hours.

She also suspected that Clint was trying to get her mind off Dennis. Ironically, it wasn't her ex-fiancé who had her insides tied up in knots, but the man with whom her brother wanted her to spend the night.

"You're an angel," Mitch said when he opened the kitchen door for her and saw the basket of food. "I'm sick of peanut butter and jelly."

"I'll cut up the leftovers and make chicken salad for sandwiches tomorrow." She stepped inside, and he relieved her of the basket.

"Don't count on leftovers. I'm starving." He set the food on the counter and started unloading, and for a ridiculous instant it annoyed her that he was so interested in the food he hadn't noticed the care she'd taken with her hair and makeup.

"Are those Maria's biscuits?" Reverently, he peeked into the foil wrapping.

"Her recipe. I made them because she has the week off."

Mitch looked at her, his mouth curving in a smile. "You look nice. And you cook. Wow."

She shook her head, but couldn't help smiling back. "You're a goof."

"Can we eat now?"

"As soon as we put the salad together."

"I'll do the chopping."

She was pleased he hadn't balked at the salad. Clint and Joe would have, but Mitch took out a red pepper and carrots from his refrigerator and added them to what she'd brought.

"Good for you," she said, watching him work on the salad. "Joe and Clint consider corn a sacrifice."

He chuckled. "I used to be that way. But ever since I got into martial arts I've tried to eat really well. Peanut butter and jelly and biscuits are definitely not the norm for me these days. Not to say I'm turning down those biscuits."

She slid him a sidelong glance, admiring the flatness

of his belly, recalling the ripple of muscle she knew lay beneath his navy blue T-shirt. "You taught karate, right?"

"For a while."

"Will you teach me?"

He'd just popped a piece of red pepper into his mouth, and frowned at her while he chewed. "Seriously?"

"I'd like to know a few self-defense moves."

"Sure, we can do that." His gaze ran down the front of her peach-colored scoop neck blouse and tan capris, lingered for a few seconds on the bare part of her legs. "I can show you some breathing exercises later. When you're dressed in something looser and more comfortable we can work on actual moves."

"Sounds good." She went back to slicing the chicken, telling herself the look meant nothing. He'd merely been assessing the suitability of her attire for a self-defense lesson. Anything else she thought she'd seen in his gaze had been wishful thinking. "By the way, Clint went into town for a haircut today and people were already talking about how you've brought in cattle."

"Good deal. Do people know it's Sugarloaf beef?"

"Clint spread it around that he and Joe sold you a small herd, and that you were getting a bull from Houston."

Mitch looked pensively out the kitchen window toward the pasture. "Any idea what the market price is for a Brahman these days?"

"Why?" That would be a long-term investment. "You're not thinking—"

"We've got company." Mitch laid down the knife and walked closer to the window. "Do you know who drives a dark blue pickup? A late model 4x4."

"No." She joined him at the window in time to see

the large truck coming slowly down the dirt road that ran along the pasture, pausing before it turned down the gravel driveway toward the house.

"It better not be that Realtor again."

"He drove a sedan."

"Yeah, I know. I'm going to run upstairs and check the monitors."

"Okay." Kate kept her gaze trained on the truck, which looked familiar the longer she stared at it. Probably nothing to worry about. It was still daylight. But then again, there was no reason to be driving that slow, as if the driver were checking out the pasture.

She washed and dried her hands, while continuing to keep tabs out the window. The truck stopped near the stone walkway to the front door. As soon as he climbed out, she recognized Brad. Though she couldn't imagine what he was doing here. Had he heard Mitch had bought the cattle and was looking for a new job?

Before Brad could reach the front door, she hurried to the staircase to warn Mitch but he was already descending two steps at a time.

"It's Brad from the Double R," she said.

"I saw him. I can't imagine what the hell he wants."

"A job maybe?"

Mitch snorted. "Or to case the place."

The thought had fleetingly crossed her mind, but she hadn't wanted to admit it. Besides, there hadn't been a rustling incident since he'd started at the Double R.

The knock at the door came. Before Mitch answered it, he asked, "Do you care if he knows you're here?"

She shrugged, curious why he'd asked. "It doesn't matter to me."

Mitch opened the door.

Brad stood with his thumbs hooked in his belt. As soon as he saw Kate, he smiled and removed his hat. He didn't seem in the least surprised to see her. Then he nodded at Mitch. "I hope you don't mind my stopping by."

"What can I do for you?" Mitch asked, unsmiling and clearly unwilling to invite him inside.

Brad fingered the brim of his hat and gestured with a tilt of his head. "You have some nice heifers out there. I heard at the post office you'd bought Sugarloaf stock. Good move."

"Glad you approve."

Kate glared at Mitch, appalled at his sarcasm.

Brad's mouth twisted wryly but he didn't seem too put off. "That should give you a real nice start."

"I'm not hiring any help at this point, if that's why you're here," Mitch said. "Sorry you came out for nothing."

Brad smiled. With his light blue eyes and dark wavy hair, he really was quite a good-looking guy. "I'm happy working at the Double R." His eyes met Kate's. "Actually, I came out here to see you."

She blinked. "Me? Why?" She glanced at Mitch's scowling face. "How did you know I was here?"

"I stopped at the Sugarloaf first and Silas told me he thought you brought Colter some supper." He smiled, displaying perfect white teeth.

"Okay," she said slowly, feeling the tension radiating from Mitch.

"I tried calling you on your cell a few times but apparently your mailbox is full."

"Oh, right, I meant to clear out those old messages."

Kate knew they were all from Dennis, and she'd hoped his inability to reach her would finally discourage him. She was counting on him being too big a coward to show up in person. "How can I help you?"

He glanced at Mitch. "Mind if we take a short walk? I have a question for you."

She started to tell him he could speak freely in front of Mitch, but one look at his sullen face and she thought better of it. "I'll be right back," she told him, and stepped outside, closing the door behind her before he said something rude.

"Normally I wouldn't intrude," Brad said, "but Silas assured me that Colter is like one of your brothers. So I figured you were just being neighborly."

"Yes," She sighed. That was the sad truth, all right. "They were best friends all through school. I was the pesky younger sister."

"Good." He grinned when she frowned. "I mean, I got the impression at Barney's the other night that he might be jealous of us shooting pool together."

"No." She adamantly shook her head. "If he looked out of sorts it was because I'd just broken off my engagement, and frankly, I'm not the type to hang out at Barney's."

"I know. I hadn't seen you there before." They silently walked a few feet on the gravel drive toward the back pasture where the cattle grazed. "Still, he didn't seem big brother protective. He was plenty ticked."

Kate rolled her eyes, but her pulse skidded. Mitch, jealous? No, couldn't be, but it was fun to fantasize. "Trust me, it's not like that."

"His loss, my gain." He walked close enough that his arm brushed hers. Funny, he was a great-looking guy, but she experienced none of the sensation she did with Mitch. "You wouldn't happen to be leaving soon, would you?"

"Uh, no, I promised to help Mitch with some light housekeeping."

"Too bad." Brad seemed genuinely disappointed. "I was hoping I could talk you into another game of pool. I'm feeling lucky. Thought I might be able to beat you this time."

Kate swallowed, nervous suddenly. Was he asking her out on a date? "I was the one who was lucky the other night. I'm really not that good."

Groaning, he placed a hand on his heart. "That was brutal. You whipped my behind."

She laughed at his mock-wounded expression. "I wouldn't say that."

He smiled, and glanced down at her pink toenails peeking out from her white strappy sandals. "I wouldn't mind a short stroll if it wouldn't bother your feet none."

She pressed her lips together. She knew darn well Mitch had gone straight to the window and hadn't missed a single move they'd made. "I should get back. We were just about to eat."

His smiled faded. "Sure. I didn't mean to butt in…." He paused. "Any chance you'd care to have supper with me some night?"

She hesitated, not knowing what to say. She didn't want to hurt his feelings but…

He shrugged. "I bet your brothers wouldn't be keen on the idea, me being just a hired hand and all."

"What? No. They would never think any such thing." The Mannings weren't snobs, for goodness' sakes.

"So maybe we could go to Barney's some evening? If not there, we could try the new place in Willowville."

Oh, boy. "The thing is, I'm really not ready to jump into the dating pool quite yet."

He gave her that Hollywood smile again. "No pressure. I don't plan on going anywhere."

"Okay," she said, smiling back. "I'll keep that in mind."

He really had gorgeous blue eyes. "Did I mention how nice you look?"

She felt the flush invade her cheeks. "Thank you." She tossed a guilty look over her shoulder, and realized they'd moved quite a ways from the house. "I really should get back before our food is cold."

"Sorry," he said, and gestured with his hat for her to precede him. "I seem to lose track of time around you."

Oh, he was a charmer, all right. She headed for the grassy strip that ran along the gravel, hoping to keep the tiny pebbles from lodging between her toes. But the grass was tall and a little scary with a bunch of creepy-crawly things that had too many hiding places. She decided the gravel wasn't so bad after all.

Brad stayed abreast of her, touching her arm in warning when she nearly stepped on a huge black beetle. "I don't envy Colter trying to get this place back in shape. He can't be planning on doing it all on his own."

She got the distinct impression the observation was more question than statement. "I honestly don't know his plans, but I expect that his father will be returning shortly."

"Is he buying more cattle?" He squinted at the small herd. "He'll need a couple of horses or a quad."

His remarks were innocuous enough, but she wasn't comfortable discussing Mitch's plans with anyone in case she slipped. "He's working something out with Clint and Joe. That's all I know," she said, picking up the pace.

It seemed Brad was ready to walk her to the door, but she purposely stopped in front of his truck. "I'll call," he said, facing her and twirling the brim of his hat in his hands. "Or, who knows, maybe we'll run into each other in town again."

"Maybe." An alarming thought occurred to her. Brad couldn't be dropping by unexpectedly like this. She'd have to clear her mailbox immediately. "If you can't reach me on my cell, you can always call the house. Or if you don't mind, leave me your number."

The pleased grin that curved his mouth made her question the wisdom of that suggestion. "Hold on. I've got a pen and paper in my glove box."

She waited nervously for him, tempted to glance toward the house. Mitch was watching. She didn't have to look to know that. And then another troubling thought occurred to her.

Brad had already scrawled his number on a piece of paper and as he rounded the hood he handed it to her. "I let some of the other guys use my phone when we're mending fences or dropping hay, so if you happen to get one of those knuckleheads, don't let them give you a hard time."

She slowly folded the paper in quarters. "How did you get my cell number?"

He gave her an unreadable glance and then shrugged a shoulder. "I bribed someone, but I'd just as soon not get them in trouble." He was all teeth again. "Go eat your supper. Give Colter my apology for keeping you so long." He hit the side of the truck and winked, before retracing his steps around the hood.

Kate hadn't missed the fact that he'd suddenly seemed anxious to leave. Made her wonder who'd given him her number. Few people around here had it. They used the ranch's landline if they wanted to contact her.

Mitch was in the kitchen slicing a tomato when she entered the house. If he'd wanted her to believe he hadn't been spying on her and Brad, he'd done a bad job since so little headway had been made on the salad.

"Sorry. I know you're starving," was all she said and immediately returned to carving the chicken. "Do you want this heated or is room temperature okay?"

"I want to know what the hell Brad was doing here."

"It won't happen again," she said, gleefully recalling that Brad had believed Mitch to be jealous. Just maybe… "I told him to call me at home if he can't get through on my cell. Plus, he gave me his number."

Mitch folded his arms across his chest and leaned back against the counter, his face darker than storm clouds. "You still haven't told me what he wanted."

"Nothing that concerns you. It's private."

He muttered a curse, following her as she carried the platter of chicken to the dining room table. "He suddenly shows up after I bring in a herd and spread it around that the Colters are back in business, and you don't think it's my concern?"

She stared at him, not sure what to think. Did his

reaction have anything to do with her at all? "He asked me out," she said. "Okay? Happy?"

"That son of a bitch." He did look jealous, and heaven help her, she was thrilled. "And you said?"

"Why, yes, of course."

_11_

STUNNED, MITCH ABSORBED the news, then calmly set down the bowl of salad and two plates. He turned to the old oak hutch for napkins. The drawer was empty. For a second he'd forgotten that most of the house had been packed up. Moved to a small cramped town house in Little Rock. What few utensils he had he'd borrowed from the Mannings, or picked up in town.

"Why?" he finally asked, when it appeared she'd offer no further explanation.

"Why go out on a date?" Kate rolled her eyes. "Sit. I'll go get the biscuits and napkins."

He followed her into the kitchen, irritated as hell that she hadn't answered him. Ignoring her, he went to the fridge telling himself he didn't need a beer so early in the evening. He got one anyway. "What do you want to drink?" he asked more gruffly than he'd intended.

"Hmm." She eyed the bottle in his hand. "I should probably have one of those, too."

"Why?" he asked, when it seemed clear she was hesitant. "I seem to recall you don't like beer."

"True, but I should get used to the taste." She smiled, looking pleased with her decision. "Yes, I will have one of those."

He grabbed a second bottle, but perversely didn't offer to get her a glass. He had a feeling he knew where this was headed, and he didn't like it one bit. She led him back to the dining room, and in spite of himself, he stared hard at her rear end, almost certain he could see the vague outline of skimpy bikini panties through the tan fabric. And damn if his cock didn't twitch.

She was not going out with Brad. No way in hell would he allow such a thing. Even if he had to warn Joe and Clint and they all ganged up on her.

"Here you go." He set the beer on the table, unopened. If she wanted to be a poolroom groupie, she could pop her own damn cap and learn to drink out of a bottle.

"Thank you." She smiled, slid onto her chair, and then used her napkin to unscrew the top.

He passed her the salad, but she motioned for him to serve himself first. Pretending not to pay attention to her, he scooped some greens onto his plate, pushed the bowl toward her and speared a chicken thigh.

"This is pretty good," she said, after taking a small sip and then studying the bottle. "I'll have to remember this brand."

He willed himself to hold his tongue and shoveled in a mouthful of salad.

"Would you pass the biscuits, please?"

He set the plate down between them, taking a biscuit and splitting it, and then slathering on too much butter. "Why Brad?"

"He's a fun, good-looking guy." She lifted a shoulder. "Why not?"

"You don't think you're rushing things?"

She frowned. "Rushing what?"

"You just broke up with Dennis."

A patronizing smile lifted her lips. "I'm just going to have dinner and play pool with him. Not have his baby." She set down her fork. "You sound an awful lot like Joe and Clint, who, by the way, better not hear about this date," she said, leveling him a stern look. "It's none of their business. You got it?"

"If Brad's planning to steal their cattle, it's their business."

"Oh, for crying out loud. He's only been around for a couple of months. Why would you think such a thing?"

"Why show up here? Now? You don't find that odd?"

Her cheeks turning pink, she regarded him with hurt in her eyes. "Can't he simply be interested in me?" she asked quietly.

Mitch lowered his gaze to his plate. Shit. How could he be such a thoughtless ass?

THE NEXT EVENING KATE brought her overnight bag with her inside the house. She wanted the option of staying and not having to drive home in the early-morning hours as she'd ended up doing last night, but more importantly, she wanted to torment Mitch. And she knew just how to go about it.

"You didn't have to knock," he said as he opened the door, his gaze going straight to the bag. "I left it unlocked."

"I know but I wanted to warn you." She handed him a sack. "Maria came back to work early. She made tortillas and carne asada."

"Bless her." Mitch opened the bag and sniffed appreciatively. "Tacos tonight."

"None for me. I ate a late lunch, but I'll keep you company after I take this bag upstairs."

"You decided to spend the night, I see." His troubled gaze went back to her satchel.

"It's okay, isn't it? We did talk about my staying."

"No, it's a good idea. As long as Clint and Joe have no problem with it."

She gave him a withering look. This crap was getting old. "Does your sister make your decisions for you?"

His obvious attempt to control a smile irritated her more. "The guest room is made up. I'll take your bag up for you."

She held it out of his reach. "I can manage, thank you."

She carried the brown leather bag up the stairs and into the guest room, and then closed the door before unpacking the two new sundresses she'd purchased in Willowville and the red one she'd found at Porter's. Oh, she'd gotten over his stupid remark during dinner last night. After rehashing it a hundred times, she'd decided nothing personal had been intended. He was focused on catching the rustlers so that's where his mind had gone when Brad showed up. Even so, she'd bet her share of the Sugarloaf that Mitch was jealous. And if he couldn't admit it to himself, she'd just have to show him.

After laying the three dresses across the bed and rating them on a scale from skimpy to downright sexy, she chose the blue, the most modest of the trio, although still risqué for her. She figured she'd ease him into the new Kate.

She quickly pulled off her jeans and T-shirt, and then took a couple of minutes to figure out how the straps were supposed to go across the back. It had seemed simple in the store with the clerk helping her, but now not so much. Maybe she'd save this one and ask Mitch to help her later. Talk about icing on the cake. She could picture his jaw hitting the floor.

The peach-colored one was easier to slip on. It was tight, though. Too bad not breathing wasn't an option. She stood in front of the small mirror and stared at the way the dress hugged every curve and dipped low between her breasts. This was so not her. Oh, how could she pull this off without tripping all over herself?

If she were Lisa, she could. Effortlessly. Lisa wouldn't think twice about wearing a dress like this and making every head turn. Kate was such a chicken she'd driven all the way to Willowville to shop in relative anonymity. Still, she thought, angling her body, it was quite a spectacular dress. If she'd been bold enough to wear something like this when she'd been with Dennis then maybe—

No. She would *not* go there. He was a jerk, and she was not in any way responsible for his poor judgment. Dennis was his own problem. Her only predicament was how to really rock this dress. She eyed the cleft between her breasts. Surely she could do better than that. She bent over and did some rearranging, and while she was down there, tousled her hair.

She straightened, stared into the mirror and smiled. Better than a push-up bra. After touching up her lip gloss, and making a few more minor adjustments, she smoothed the silky fabric over her tummy and reminded herself to keep it sucked in. At this point, she didn't think she could handle a single bite of a taco. It would all be worth it once she saw Mitch's face.

HE PREPARED EXTRA TACO fixings in case Kate changed her mind, and then carried the food to the table. He skipped the beer and brought the pitcher of tea. Damn, but he felt like a babysitter trying to set a good example. Not that he'd even mention the word around her. She'd be liable to take his head off. He didn't blame her, except he also knew that Kate wasn't acting like herself. Going out with someone like that hustler Brad? Hell, talk about asking for trouble. Mitch knew the type too well. In his younger days, he'd been no angel himself.

Realizing he'd forgotten the salsa, he returned to the kitchen. He reentered the dining room the same time as she came down the stairs. He had to look twice. If he hadn't let her in himself, he wasn't sure he'd have recognized her.

"I hope you weren't waiting for me," she said, her gaze going to the table, a hand to her belly. "I couldn't possibly eat a thing."

He could see why. The dress had to have been sprayed on. "You going somewhere?" he asked, trying like hell not to stare at her chest, at the way her breasts plumped up over the neckline of her dress. Damn, it wasn't a neckline. It wasn't anywhere near her neck.

"Not right now."

"Then why are you all gussied up?"

"I wanted your opinion."

He pulled out a chair and focused his entire attention on sitting down. Was she looking for a reaction? Well, she got one. He just wasn't keen on her seeing it. "Opinion on what?"

"The dress." She turned around and paused, glancing over her shoulder at him. "Well?"

The front was low cut, the back was almost nonexistent. It formed a V to her waist, leaving an expanse of bare silky skin. The skirt ended at midthigh. "It's kind of short."

She faced him and then glanced down at her legs. "It's summer. The styles are shorter," she said matter-of-factly. "I picked up some bronzing lotion when I went shopping today. My back and legs will look better with a little more color."

They looked damn good now. He poured tea for each of them, and then concentrated on scooping meat and diced tomato onto corn tortillas.

"Well? You didn't tell me what you think."

He looked up just as she fiddled with the front of her dress, exposing more of her right breast. If she tugged one more inch it would be all over for him. He went back to making his taco. "It's nice, I guess."

"That wasn't very enthusiastic."

He made the mistake of glancing up. Her lips were formed in a cute pout, and her nipples were as hard as he was. "Aren't you—cold?"

"It's eighty-six degrees."

"Not in here."

She sighed loudly. "Maybe you'll like the next one better."

"Next one?"

"I bought three. I'm trying to decide which one to wear first."

He quit pretending interest in his dinner and leaned back. "Where?"

"On my date with Brad," she said breezily. "You're a guy. I figured you could tell me which one he'd like best."

Was she that naive, or was she trying to make him mad? "What happened to 'it's just a game of pool, you're not having his baby?'"

She planted a hand on her hip, causing a slight jiggling action he found hard to ignore. "Your point would be?"

"Wear that thing and in nine months you might be having more than a bad day."

She laughed. "We're going to dinner first. I want to look nice."

He pointedly stared at the short hem. "You can't play pool in that."

"Yes, Dad." She turned and headed for the stairs. "Eat while I change into the next one."

He almost told her not to bother, that he'd seen enough. Enough to make him suffer through another frustrated night. But as he watched her hips sway from side to side, his gaze lowering to the long lean curves of her calves, his heartbeat surged with anticipation.

She wanted his opinion. He'd give her one, all right. After the fashion show. But she wasn't going to like it.

"THIS ONE MIGHT BE my favorite." She did a small twirl after she left the stairs. "Although I'm partial to red. What do you think?"

That he'd probably bust his fly before the night was over. He looked her up and down, lingering on the triangular cutout that went from her navel to her breasts. The dress was just as short as the other one, the neckline low and scalloped, and the back another huge cutout that exposed the delicate curve of her spine and ended just above the swell of her backside. "Is saving on material the new trend?"

Kate chuckled. "It's surprisingly comfortable. And cool. Almost feels as if I have nothing on."

A chunk of meat seemed to lodge in his throat. He took a big gulp of iced tea and stared down at his empty plate. Funny, he barely recalled eating.

"I don't know," she said thoughtfully staring down at her legs. "Do you think it's shorter than the other one?" Slowly, she turned and then after presenting her back, looked over her shoulder at him. "Tell me the truth. Do I have too many freckles to wear something like this?"

He let his gaze roam the smooth, even expanse of her back and shoulders. Where he lived in Florida, most of the women were tanned, often overdoing it. He couldn't recall the last time he'd seen such creamy, soft-looking skin. He wanted to touch her. "No. You look very—"

"Very what?"

His honesty would only encourage her. "If I were you, I'd think twice about going out on a date in that dress."

Her eyes widened and she abruptly faced him. "Why? Does it make me look fat?"

He choked back a laugh. "No. You want me to be candid, right?"

"Absolutely." She pulled out a chair across from him, and plopped down. She had to be doing that jiggling thing on purpose, knowing that it drove him nuts. But then why would she? She'd been annoyingly treating him as if he were one of her girlfriends.

"Then I'll put it this way, you wear something like that and you'll have five guys lining up to buy you drinks and pestering you the entire night."

She waved him off. "Not if I'm with Brad."

Hell, if he heard that name one more time he was going to lose it. At this point, nothing would make him happier than to find out the guy was a thief. He'd personally escort him to prison.

"I've got a question." Mitch could feel his temper edging dangerously up a notch. "What kind of guy shows up here to talk to you not knowing whether we're seeing each other?"

She gave him a perplexed look. "Everyone knows you're like a brother to me."

Shit. He passed a hand over his face. "The locals, yeah, but Brad doesn't know differently."

"He asked around."

A sudden headache throbbed at Mitch's temples. Great. He had a whole night of surveillance ahead of him. "Anyway, that doesn't matter. You were engaged until a lousy five minutes ago. You're vulnerable. What kind of man takes advantage of the situation?"

"Are you trying to tell me I shouldn't go out with him?" she asked idly, adding a second sprig of mint to her glass, before taking a sip. She put the glass down, leaving a sheen of moisture on her lower lip, which she dabbed at with the tip of her tongue, and then expectantly met his eyes.

"You have to ask?"

She shrugged, unconcerned, and pushed back from the table. "He'll be a pleasant distraction. That's all. I have one last dress to show you, then we can decide."

He clenched his jaw as he watched her ascend the stairs, exposing far too much skin. Was she deliberately trying to goad him? Flaunt the fact that she didn't have to listen to him any more than she did Joe and Clint? That was the only explanation for her behavior. Okay, so he deserved it. Well, not this. No red-blooded man deserved this, but he had done his share of babying her. It was a hard thing to stop, and he wasn't all that sure why. He'd thought a lot about it, too. Last night, he'd even considered the notion that the reason he couldn't stop treating her like a sister was that if he did, if he treated her like the woman she was, there would be no stopping him from seducing her right out of those ridiculous dresses.

He needed to distance himself from her, especially since she was spending the nights with him. And because she deserved so much better than him. Granted, anyone, with the exception of Brad, would have been a giant improvement over Dennis, but Mitch was fully aware that he was no good for Kate. She needed someone she could count on. Who would be there for her no matter what. Not him. No way. Not him.

Picking up plates and utensils, he scraped back from the table, and then stalked to the kitchen. He had a good mind to tell her he was done being her audience. She could choose any damn dress she pleased. She looked hot in all of them. Is that what she wanted to hear? Was she still pissed over his remark about Brad using her to gain information?

Yep, that made sense. He'd been an ass last night, and it was up to him to make things better. She needed to hear that she was beautiful and sexy. Which she was, in spades, but she needed to hear it from him. He wasn't about to tell her the unvarnished truth, however. So, what would both stroke her ego, and keep him from crossing the line? It would help a lot if whatever he did dissuaded her from going out with Brad. Okay, no pressure.

Act naturally was what he needed to do. Naturally for a man who didn't get hard at the very thought of her. And in that vein, he filled the sink with sudsy water and submerged the plates along with everything else, even a couple of glasses he hadn't used yet. He went to work, washing, whistling and waiting for her to show up in another torturous dress. A couple minutes later, he heard the click of high heels on the hardwood floor behind him.

High heels?

In spite of himself, he twisted around. He vaguely noticed the dress had blue flowers on it, but his gaze went straight to her legs. On her feet were heels, all right. About three-inch spikes that did incredible things to her already toned legs. His mouth went dry. He jerked back from his wayward thoughts and splashed the front of his jeans.

He muttered a curse, and glanced down at his thickening fly.

"What happened?" She ripped a couple of paper towels from the dispenser and approached as if she wanted to help him dry off.

He pressed up against the counter. "Nothing. I'm washing dishes."

"I see that." Her right strap slipped off her shoulder. She reached to tug it in place, and the entire dress seemed to slide a few inches down her body. With lightning reflexes, she jerked up the front. "I need help with the zipper," she explained. "And the straps."

She angled around to show him. The dress gaped open all the way down to her red silk panties.

"Shit." He snatched his hand from the sudsy water.

Several drops of blood dripped from the side of his finger.

"What?" She hurried over to him and saw that he'd cut himself. "Mitch." Her eyes worried, she used one of the towels to blot the wound. "You put a knife in there?"

"Yeah, stupid, I know." He hadn't been paying attention. "It's no big deal." Moving the paper towel, he looked closer at the small slice, relieved to see it really wasn't anything serious. "I've had worse paper cuts."

She gave him a bland look. "Yes, Mr. Macho. All the same we need to tape it up." Her gaze darted around while she still clutched the front of her dress, and then met his eyes with a frustrated sigh. "You need two hands to zip me, and I need two hands to doctor you."

He pursed his lips to keep from smiling. "What happens if you let go?" The words were out of his mouth before the stupidity of them registered.

She didn't even blink. Her eyes glittered with something he was too much a coward to analyze, and then her hand relaxed. "Shall we find out?"

12

KATE HELD HER BREATH. The fire in his eyes was worth every shred of indignity and self-doubt she'd suffered to put on this little show. For the first time she totally got that he was interested. In her. He could say what he wanted, or hide behind that impassive mask he liked to wear, but she knew better.

"Look, Katie, I was only teasing. I didn't mean—" He looked down at his injured hand. Just for a moment, but when he lifted his gaze, the mask was back in place.

Too late. She wasn't buying it. "You're lying."

His brows dipped in disbelief, and then he slowly wrapped the paper towel around his finger.

"Want me to tell you how I know?"

He drew his attention away from his inept attempt at first aid, and studied her with narrowed eyes. "Knock yourself out."

"You called me Katie. You do that when you want to push me away emotionally. Or to remind me that I'm Joe and Clint's little sister in your eyes. Wait. That's not quite right. You're actually reminding yourself, aren't you?"

Annoyance flashed across his face. "I don't need reminding."

"Hmm. Could've fooled me." She smiled, moved

closer. Close enough to see fear flicker in his gray eyes. Close enough that he shifted. "Don't be so jumpy."

"You're gonna stand there playing psychoanalyst while I bleed to death?"

"I thought you've had worse paper cuts." She laughed at his scowl, and then used her free hand to maneuver a peek under the paper towel. It didn't seem too bad. "Tell you what…I'll go take off this dress, and then bandage you up." She hesitated, purposely letting the front of the dress slip low enough to expose the tops of her breasts. "Keep pressure on that until I get back."

She lifted her gaze, pleased to see his centered right where she'd planned. He could argue all he wanted that he wasn't interested, but that was plain horse pucky. The only problem with this game, which she'd started, was that she was getting a bit too hot and bothered herself.

What if she did drop the dress? Stood here in nothing but bikini panties. He'd already seen her in a see-through teddy, although the room had been semidark. She couldn't imagine what he'd do. Turn his back? Order her to cover up? Pull her into his arms and kiss her until she couldn't breathe? She voted for the last option. Except her vote didn't count.

And then, too, did she have the nerve?

Sadly, she didn't. Not here in the kitchen, anyway. She could only pretend to be Lisa to a certain point without totally humiliating herself. Besides, once that line was crossed, their relationship would change forever.

She cleared her throat, and stepped back, regaining her hold on the bodice. "Okay, then. I'll be right back." She almost forgot she'd put on the heels and nearly lost her footing when she spun around too quickly.

"Wait."

She stopped, her exposed back to him, wondering where her confidence had gone. Until a second ago she'd been in the zone, empowered by the knowledge that she'd gotten to him, that he couldn't hide his attraction. For several glorious minutes, she *had* been Lisa and she could do anything.

Kate breathed in deeply and then turned back to him, despising the fear that she struggled to choke down.

"You're wrong, Kate," he said, coming toward her.

Her heart slammed into her chest, but to her amazement, her voice sounded normal when she asked, "About?"

One side of his mouth quirked up a smidgen. "I think I can handle that zipper. Turn around."

"Good." She did as he asked, closing her eyes once he couldn't see her face, and praying for composure. So, he wasn't going to challenge her observation. A part of her was greatly relieved. "Don't hurt your finger," she said unnecessarily and then mentally kicked herself.

"Have you got a free hand?"

"Sure." She reached around, and he took her hand and placed it at the bottom of the zipper.

His warm moist breath danced over her shoulder, and then down her spine as he pushed the fabric together. "What do you do with these straps?"

"Um, I might need help with those, too."

He didn't answer.

"After we get a bandage on your finger, that is. But if that's a problem, I'll figure it out later." She bit her lower lip as his hand brushed her back, horribly afraid she'd break out in a bunch of unattractive goose bumps.

She tried not to move, hoping he'd hurry, hoping he

wouldn't. The heat from his body had pushed her own temperature up several degrees, and her breasts had started to ache, her hardened nipples so sensitive that even the slinky fabric caused an unbearable friction.

"If this is too difficult, I can—"

"Nope." Mitch grazed her fanny. With his arm? His hips? His—?

"Hold still. I've almost got it."

She had been holding still. Perfectly still. Hadn't she? "This is crazy. I should just go change."

"Here we go." He cupped his hand over her shoulder, and she jumped when she felt the dress constrict around her.

She stared down at the bodice, so much tighter now than when she'd tried the sundress on at the store. Her tender breasts felt as though they would spill out of the top, and her nipples were entirely too visible.

"The straps are going to be tricky, and I don't want to get any blood on your dress." He moved his hand from her shoulder. "Turn around. Let's see."

There was nothing to do but comply. She faced him, her hands fisted at her sides.

His gaze went directly to her chest. He blinked, and quickly switched his attention lower, and gave her a vague once-over. "Nice." His voice was wrong. A bit hoarse. "The medicine cabinets are empty, but I have a first aid kit in my truck."

Kate didn't mind that he left, rather quickly, out the kitchen door. She welcomed the brief reprieve. Now that she'd gotten his attention, where did they go from here? Lisa would probably suggest that they bang each other's brains out and get the matter over with so they could move on. Kate wasn't that brazen. There wasn't enough tequila in Texas to blurt out something like that.

Maybe it was time for her to pull back. Skip the games and the taunting. Try to act naturally, and see if he'd pick up the reins. Frankly, she didn't see there was much left to do. She certainly didn't want to jeopardize his surveillance efforts. Or their relationship. Besides, she wasn't in her right mind. That had to be the reason she was playing games to begin with. Normal, sensible Kate didn't toy with men, and certainly didn't try to drive a man crazy.

She tugged at the front of her dress, looking for relief from the snug fit. Glancing down, it occurred to her that she should've used the opportunity to visit the bathroom and make sure everything was where it was supposed to be. Maybe it wasn't too late.

His truck was parked outside the garage and easily seen from the dining room window. She stopped for a quick peek, but saw no sign of him. Ducking her head, she tried to figure out if he might be sitting inside the cab, but she was quite sure he wasn't. She waited awhile, half expecting him to enter through one of the doors. Five minutes later, she stood there alone, staring out into the growing darkness, panic rising in her throat.

HE HAD TO GO BACK INSIDE at some point. Even if he used the lame excuse that he'd found nothing in his truck and had to check the barn, she'd know it wouldn't have taken this long to find a lousy bandage. She'd know that she'd really gotten to him. But at least she wouldn't be staring at the damn proof.

For the third time Mitch adjusted his jeans. Time

had reduced the snugness, but not enough. All bets were off the moment he'd laid eyes on her. Worst of all, he didn't understand the intensity of his reaction. Sure, she looked hot in those dresses, and Kate had turned into quite the beauty. But frankly, he'd been surrounded by beautiful women since he'd left Texas. First, in the entertainment industry, and even now, working as a private pilot for Winston Spelling.

Women flocked to the billionaire, and the old guy liked having the assortment of eye candy hovering around his five mansions. To his credit, Spelling wasn't one to drop his bucket in every well. He just liked women in general. As a result, Mitch had never been short on feminine company. He was damn lucky in that department, but that made his unwise attraction to Kate all the more confusing.

If anything, he should be staying as far away from her as possible. Out of respect for Clint and Joe, if nothing else. So he was attracted to her, and it seemed the feelings went both ways. He wasn't a horny kid who couldn't keep his dick in his pants.

He walked around the sadly empty barn, expending pent-up energy, kicking at clumps of hay and disturbing the packed dirt. It was starting to get dark and although it was too early to worry about stationing himself at the monitors, he was going to walk into the house and go straight up the stairs. She'd follow him, but that was okay. She'd settle down once they were working.

Hell, he was the one who needed to settle down. He stretched out his neck and then his back, did a couple of squats. His finger throbbed some, but the pressure from the bandage he'd wrapped around it helped. He opened his fist and stared at the foil package in his hand. The condom had been next to the first aid kit in the glove compartment. He should've left the damn thing right there. He had no business even carrying it into the house. He wasn't going to need it. Nope. Not here. Not with Kate.

After shadowboxing a few minutes, and then employing a couple of karate moves, concentrating on a clearly visualized groin kick, he headed out of the barn and toward the front door. Kate was standing on the porch. She still wore the blue dress and high heels. The image of her bare back and red panties assaulted him. As did the memory of how badly he'd wanted to taste her, lick a path all the way down her spine to her fleshy cheeks. He'd wanted to touch his tongue to her hardened nipples, feel them against his naked chest.

He should probably tell her to take the night off. Put some distance between them. But she'd likely use the time to go out with Brad, and that thought Mitch couldn't stomach. After all, he'd promised Clint he'd keep an eye on her.

KATE SAW HIM LEAVE the barn and head toward the house. She lifted the hand she'd had pressed to her belly and waved when it looked as if he was going to swing around to the back. But then she realized he'd already seen her. That he'd wanted to avoid her. The knowledge stung at first, and then she realized that was probably a good thing.

She waited until he reached the porch and the shadows weren't concealing his face. "You've been gone awhile. I was worried."

He showed her his wrapped finger. "I found the first

aid kit in my truck but then I thought I saw someone hanging around the barn."

"Oh, no." That, she hadn't expected.

"It was nothing," he said quickly. "I checked. Probably a stray cat."

She glanced toward the barn. "We should set up motion detectors."

"Good idea. I'll pick some up tomorrow." He swatted at a moth drawn to the inside light, and then held open the screen door.

"I haven't been upstairs to check the monitors," she said, glancing over her shoulder at him as she went over the threshold. His gaze was on her backside, trapping her between self-conscious and thrilled. "I figured we were safe until dark."

"I agree. All the attacks happened after midnight, which makes sense, but I don't want to get complacent." He closed the screen door, and then the heavy oak one behind him, taking his time before he faced her.

"I see you didn't need my help," she said, indicating his bandaged finger.

"It stopped bleeding. Seems I'll live."

"Good. Death by washing dishes would've made for a heck of an obituary."

He gave her a wry smile. "Guess I better finish what I was doing."

"Everything is washed, dried and put away."

"You didn't have to, but thanks." He slid a look out the front window, and then drew the curtains on both sides. "No sense being on display."

Her gaze drifting toward the windows, she shivered, thinking someone could be out there watching them.

"I've always felt so safe out here. I've never locked my car, and we just recently started locking the house."

"I didn't mean to spook you. The rustlers aren't interested in us, just the cattle." He moved to the next window and adjusted the parted curtains.

"Yes, but anyone casing the place would have to wonder what I'm doing here every night."

"True." He gave her such a long, measuring look it brought on another shiver. "Come here."

"What?" She followed him to the next window, and then waited for him to close the curtains.

Instead, he took her hand and pulled her toward him. She tilted her head back to look into his eyes, and he smiled, fleetingly, before he claimed her mouth. His lips were gentle and coaxing, as he let go of her hand, slid his arms around her and ran his palm up her back to her nape.

For a second she didn't fully appreciate what was happening, wasn't convinced that out of her desperate longing she hadn't dreamed this kiss. But his lips firmed as his mouth slanted and his insistent hands drew her so close she felt his arousal against her quivering belly.

She parted her lips, and he swept his tongue into her mouth. He tasted spicy and minty at the same time, and she hoped it was the sweet tea that he tasted from her and not the childish amazement weaving through her, thrilling her, making her giddy. She was kissing Mitch. No, even more astonishing, *he* was kissing *her.*

Before she was ready for the kiss to end, he pulled back and gazed down at her. "If anyone is watching, they don't have to wonder what you're doing here."

"I don't think that was convincing enough."

His brows went up. "Is that right?"

"Too tame."

"Ah."

"If anyone is out there, I think we should really give them a show."

He looked as if he was trying not to smile. "I'll follow your lead."

If that was a dare, he didn't know her as well as he thought he did. She smiled, and reached for his belt buckle.

He tensed, all amusement gone from his face. "What are you doing?"

"Relax," she whispered, "or you'll ruin everything. Kiss me."

He hauled her against him, so tight she had no choice but to abandon the buckle. Her nipples were hard, his erection even harder. He took her earlobe between his teeth and lightly bit her. "This isn't a good idea," he whispered raggedly.

"Mugging for the camera, so to speak?"

He nipped the skin below her ear, and then pressed a kiss on the same spot. "You know what I mean."

"Right." She put her arms around him and yanked the hem of his shirt from the waistband of his jeans. "We should be doing this in private."

"We shouldn't be doing this, period." Despite his words, he found her lips again and pushed his tongue deep into her mouth.

She arched against him, pressing her breasts to his broad strong chest, the pressure producing a frisson of pleasure that tingled through her. Instinctively she moved her hips, rubbing herself against his rock-hard penis. He moaned into her mouth and cupped her bottom. But he didn't stop her. Just dug his fingers into her fleshy cheeks, his heartbeat so strong and fast she could feel it vibrate off her breast.

She so wanted to be naked with him, skin to skin, feel his muscled chest against her aching nipples. She wanted his hot mouth on her, everywhere, doing wickedly intimate things that would leave an imprint so deep she'd relive the sensations for nights to come.

Almost as if he'd read her mind, he broke the kiss and briefly concentrated on the sensitive skin at the side of her neck. His lips trailed to her collarbone, and then he ran the tip of his tongue along the top of her right breast, tracing the cut of her dress.

The sudden thought that there really could be someone out there watching them momentarily stole her pleasure. "Close the curtains," she whispered.

"Hmm?" he murmured absently, continuing his trek, dipping his tongue beneath the silky fabric.

"The curtains."

He seemed to sober as he drew away from her, his gaze flickering to the window. Twilight cloaked the landscape, a few salmon-colored clouds streaming over the horizon, the only remnants of sunset.

"If someone is out there, I think they get the picture," she said jokingly, but it was too late. She could almost see the barrier go up between them. He hadn't just pulled away to close the curtains, he'd mentally withdrawn.

"I was out of line." He seemed to find it hard to look at her. "I'm sorry."

"I didn't say that because I wanted you to stop." She swallowed a lump of disappointment because she knew there wasn't anything she could do or say to recapture those few minutes of bliss. "I only wanted to take this upstairs. I don't want anything to stop. I want—I want—" Why couldn't she just say it? Because she knew he was about to reject her, no matter what she said or even if she begged, and *that* she couldn't take.

His expression softened, and lifting a hand, he touched her cheek. "It's better this way, Kate, trust me."

"I don't." She shook her head. "Not about this. I know you're attracted to me. It's not my imagination. So I can only assume this has to do with some misguided sense of loyalty to my brothers."

His laugh sounded strangled. "Yes, I'm attracted to you. I obviously couldn't lie about that even if I wanted to."

The admission pleased her, boosted her courage. "I'm missing the point," she said with purpose, twice as pleased now because she sounded so much like Lisa.

"I know you can't see how fragile you are right now, Kate. I know that, but this is where you do have to trust me."

Uh, trust him? She wanted to smack him. He didn't know her nearly as well as he thought he did. "Fine." She threw up her hands. "You're right. Why risk our friendship? Things are just peachy the way they are."

His face creased in a skeptical frown. "You're angry."

"I understand you're trying to be noble. It's fine."

"Kate, nobility has nothing to do with it."

"No, really, you're right." She gave him a sweet smile. "I'm sure Brad is about all I can handle, anyway."

The murderous expression on Mitch's face made her

jerk back. But she quickly schooled her own expression to something flirtatious and unaffected. If he didn't want her going out with Brad, then he'd damn well better do something to stop her.

13

ONLY FOUR NIGHTS HAD PASSED since Kate had put on that show and he'd nearly compromised every principle that still mattered to him.

And yet, here he was, in the dim light, watching her sleep. Curled up on her side, she hugged the pillow, knees drawn to her chest, her tempting derriere sticking out close to the edge of his sister's old bed. The hem of her baggy khaki shorts had ridden up on one thigh, giving him a narrow peek of pink lacy panties. He should've been watching the monitors.

One stinking week since he'd brought the cattle over and already his patience was wearing thin. It wasn't that he'd expected the rustlers to instantly jump at the bait, or that he was anxious to return to Palm Beach or his job. Spending so much time with Kate was getting to him.

He pinched the bridge of his nose and stifled a yawn. *Now* he was starting to get tired when he still had two hours of surveillance left? Great. She'd taken the first shift before turning the task over to him at one-thirty. A waste of her time as it turned out because he hadn't slept at all up until that point. Not even for ten minutes. He resented that it had been so easy for her to shut everything out. And so damn quickly. She hadn't even made it to her room. She'd sat at the edge of the bed to chat for a few minutes and the next thing he knew she was sound asleep.

He'd been a fool for not waking her right away and sending her to the guest room. Instead, he'd tormented himself by watching her for the past two hours. And wondering how long he'd be able to hold out and not carry her to his bed. Not tonight, and not tomorrow or the night after. He had at least that much self-control in reserve, and she'd been cooperative by not taunting him with skimpy dresses or casual touches that meant more to him than they should. But he was no saint, and sooner or later the discipline he'd prided himself in wouldn't be enough.

Kate rolled over and looked blearily at him. "Is that you?"

He straightened, glad she looked too out of it to realize he'd been staring. "You fell asleep."

"I know," she murmured, and blinked. "That noise— Is that your cell phone?"

With a start, he realized he'd been so preoccupied he hadn't heard the distinctive ring tone. He dug into his pocket, wondering who the hell would be calling at this time of night, and hoping it wasn't an emergency. The second before he checked the caller ID he knew who it was, and he doubted an emergency was involved. It wouldn't occur to his boss's daughter that she might be disturbing him, and as much as he'd like to ignore the call, he knew she wouldn't give up. Besides, she'd already left two messages he hadn't gotten around to returning.

"Hello?" He scanned the monitors, assuring himself all was well outside, and then glanced at Kate.

She seemed more alert, even a bit anxious. No surprise,

since Clint had left for Hawaii earlier in the day and now a late-night call.

As he got to his feet, Mitch gave her a sign that everything was okay, and then he headed to the hall for privacy. "Yeah, Baby, I'm here.

"Mitch." Savannah Spelling was drunk. Not slurring-her-words smashed, but enough to disappoint Mitch, make him wonder what kind of mess she'd gotten into this time. "I miss you. When are you coming home?"

"Do you know what time it is?"

"In Palm Beach, or in that awful place you insist on being?"

"Where are you, Baby?"

"Do you care?" she asked petulantly. The nickname Baby had been with her since childhood and couldn't be more appropriate. She was twenty-one, going on thirteen, and as spoiled as they came.

"You know I do."

"Prove it and come home."

Mitch sighed, ducking a look through the open door at the monitors. He couldn't see Kate, but hoped she'd fallen back to sleep. "I'm not finished here."

"Can't you get someone else to do whatever it is you're doing? I hate being here without you."

"I know, but this can't be helped. Tell me where you are."

"At home. Bored out of my mind. Happy?"

"You should try to get some rest."

"Boooring." She drew out the word and then yawned. "It's not just me. Dad wants you to come back to work."

"He's still out of the country, Baby," Mitch said and then let silence lapse. She'd nodded off on him before, and it wouldn't be a bad thing if she did now. He felt sorry for the kid, and he'd always tried his best to keep an eye on her, but she was a handful and not his responsibility.

"Mitch?"

He briefly closed his eyes and stretched his neck to the side. "I'm here, Baby."

"I hate it when you're not around." Her voice was softer now, and she was repeating herself. A good sign she'd soon be down for the count.

"Are you in bed?"

"Yes."

"Pull the covers up to your chin."

She sighed wearily. "Okay."

He smiled sadly at the sound of her childlike voice. Her father was such a great man in so many ways, but a lousy parent, who couldn't see how much she craved his attention. "Pretend I'm tucking you in."

She yawned into the phone. "Will you call me tomorrow?"

"I promise I'll call. Sweet dreams, Baby." He waited for her to disconnect first, and then turned off his phone and slid it into his pocket.

He hated thinking about how many jams he'd helped Baby out of, or the times she'd cried on his shoulder after a broken relationship. It wasn't going to be easy leaving her and moving back to Texas.

The sudden thought nearly knocked him off his feet. He didn't plan on leaving Palm Beach. Not for good. He liked his job, the freedom it afforded him, the travel, the great money…. His gaze was drawn to the rustic walls and beams that had been home for eighteen years but was so remote from his life now. His problem was that he couldn't stand the thought of the ranch being sold. He needed this place to be Colter land, to be there when he yearned for home and a simpler life. If he could just take care of the rustling problem, his parents would come back and things would be right again. His plan had to work, damn it. It had to.

KATE PRETENDED TO BE ASLEEP when he reentered the room. It wasn't easy keeping perfectly still when she felt like the worst kind of fool. She'd overheard everything, or at least enough to know that he had someone waiting for him back in Florida. The knowledge nearly squeezed the life out of her. Why hadn't he just told her? She would've backed off. Saved herself a good dose of humiliation.

If it were anyone else but Mitch, she would think that he'd been playing with her, amusing himself with her hapless taunting. Yet she had no clue why he hadn't admitted being involved with someone. She'd come out and asked him, and he'd denied it. Maybe she didn't know him as well as she thought she did. People changed all the time. Hadn't she been convinced she knew Dennis?

The depressing thought was the final straw. No way was she going to stay here and fake sleeping. At the moment, she wasn't crazy about being in the same room with him. She opened her eyes and found him staring at her.

"I'm sorry the phone woke you." He reclaimed the chair in front of the monitors, no trace of guilt or discomfort in his demeanor. "Why don't you go to your room and try to sleep for as long as you can?"

She sat up, baffled, because if he knew she was awake, he had to know she'd overheard. Shouldn't he have been a tad sheepish? "Who was that?" she asked unabashedly, not even caring how impolite the question.

"My boss's daughter."

"At—" Kate glanced at her watch "—three-thirty in the morning."

"The young lady has a problem with boundaries," he said drily, turning away to watch the monitors.

Kate stewed, contemplating leaving. Curiosity won. "You should have told me."

He turned back to her with narrowed eyes. "Told you what?"

"That you had a girlfriend."

He snorted. "If I had one, I would've told you and saved us both a lot of headache."

Screw him. She scooted to the edge of the bed, noticing how high her shorts had risen only when she saw his gaze flicker to her legs. An hour ago she would've used the situation to tempt him. She tugged the cargo khakis down to midthigh. "I'm wide-awake at this point if you want me to take over the monitors."

He shook his head, watching intently as she slipped her feet into her sandals. "I'm not sure what you heard, but clearly you've got the wrong idea."

Right. Kate pressed her lips together. He'd called the woman *baby* for God's sake. Even the word *sweetheart* she could've forgiven as more generic. Still annoying, but tolerable.

"I'll be in the guest room. As soon as it's light I'm going to head home. I've got some errands to run."

"Kate."

She hadn't expected him to follow, and he startled her in the hall. "You should be watching the monitors."

"There's a lot of things I should be doing." He pulled her into his arms and kissed her.

She started to object, but he took advantage of her parted lips and stroked his tongue into her mouth, slow and deep, until she helplessly responded. He ran his hand down her back in a gentle caress until he reached her bottom, and then he cupped her fanny, hauling her against his arousal.

Somewhere in the back of her mind she knew this was crazy, that she should push him away. But she couldn't seem to muster the strength, mentally or physically. He had come to her. There had been no games, no lame attempts at seduction. She couldn't imagine what her hair looked like after having just awoken. He didn't seem to care. He'd come because he wanted her. She tasted his need in his kiss, felt his determination in the strong steady beat of his heart against her breast.

She touched his tongue with hers, heady from the warm smell of his skin, from the heat of his body where it pressed intimately against hers. He used his free hand to brush a wayward lock of hair away from her face, and then stroked her cheek with the pad of his thumb.

Kate tilted her head back and gazed at him through unfocused eyes. "Mitch, the monitors."

He groaned, pulled her tighter against him, his body shuddering at the pressure. "You feel so damn good." He kissed her again, hard, his beard-stubbled jaw rasping against her overly sensitized skin. "But you're right."

Selfishly, she wished she hadn't reminded him. Damn her sense of responsibility. Only she could've been thinking of surveillance at a time like this.

"Come back to the room with me," he whispered, caressing her back.

She nodded, swallowing hard. "But we need to talk."

"All right." He searched her face, brushed another kiss across her lips and then took her hand and led her back to his sister's old room.

The dim reflection from the monitors painted the room a murky gray. The closed curtains ensured privacy but blocked out the moonlight. Still, she was glad she could see his face, for all the good it would do her. If the man wanted to conceal his thoughts, he was a master at masking his expression.

As soon as they'd checked the screens and found that everything was okay near the pens, she perched uneasily at the foot of the bed. Mitch pulled the oak spindle-back chair away from the monitors and angled it toward her before sitting, his long legs only inches from hers.

Was it a bad idea for her to stay? Maybe unconsciously she'd reminded him about the monitors because she needed the chance to think. Or at least stop mindlessly reacting. But it hardly mattered. Just because contact had been broken didn't mean his kiss hadn't stayed on her lips. Even the warmth between her thighs hadn't dissipated. Staring at him didn't help. She was really liking the shadowed-jaw look.

He gave her a heart-melting smile and reached for her hand.

"Oh, no. We talk first." She folded her arms across her chest. "You can't kiss me like you did and not tell me who she is."

"I already told you. She's my boss's daughter." His gaze never wavered from hers. "Definitely not my girlfriend. Baby's only twenty-one."

"Baby?"

"Her name's really Savannah but everyone calls her Baby. Like in the movie. And appropriately so. She's spoiled and still acts like a kid."

Kate paused. She didn't normally jump to conclusions, but where Mitch was concerned, there was nothing "normal" about it. "I'm sorry. Apparently I—"

"When I first started working for her father she hit on me. She was too young, *and* my boss's daughter so I squashed that real quick."

"I'm surprised she didn't retaliate."

He shrugged. "I think she ended up appreciating that I showed restraint. The girl is drop-dead gorgeous and rich. She can pretty much have anyone she wants, but it's the classic case of simply wanting her father's attention."

Kate sighed. Mitch lived in a totally different world now, one she couldn't begin to fathom. First a popular television actress and now a beautiful rich girl. He had it made. Why would he even bother looking at plain and simple Kate?

"We're friends now," he continued. "Although that's not an apt description. It's more like, if she gets into trouble, she comes to me. I've tried to get her to quit drinking and even talked her into going to therapy. The main thing is, I think she's glad that it's not about sex between us. End of story."

Relief swept through Kate, so swiftly and physically she had to brace herself on the bed. He didn't have someone else. When he'd kissed her, he'd meant it. She loved that he wanted her. She wanted him. Badly.

The next step, though, had to be thought out, had to

be smart. Of all the things she was feeling then, smart wasn't one of them.

"Well, I've distracted you enough," she said as she stood, her gaze deliberately staying on the monitor and away from him. "I'm going to get a couple hours sleep and—"

"Kate." He caught her hand, refusing to release her when she tried to tug free. "Don't you believe me?"

"No, that's not it. I mean, it's nothing. You have to watch the monitors, and I should get some sleep."

"Look at me."

She breathed in deeply, and then forced herself to meet his troubled gaze.

"You don't get a pass on this one. Tell me what's wrong."

She stared down at their joined hands. "I've shamelessly taunted you, and I'm embarrassed. Happy?"

He snorted. "Actually, yeah. I thought you were upset because I'd kissed you."

She studied his expression. He wasn't teasing. A trace of relief lingered in his eyes. "You know me better than that by now," she said wryly. Hadn't she practically thrown herself at him from the moment he'd arrived? The memory of that first awful night lit up like a bonfire in her mind. Not something she was keen on recalling, and yet her body reacted in ways that weren't embarrassed at all.

He smiled and gave her hand another tug. "Then why are you running away?"

She let him pull her toward him, placing her hands on his shoulders when he slid his arms around her waist. He gazed up at her with such tenderness that she actually got weak in the knees. She lifted a hand and lightly combed her fingers through his hair, pleased when his eyes drifted closed and his nostrils flared.

She sagged against him, and he tightened his arms around her before shifting and pulling her onto his lap. Laughing nervously, Kate struggled a bit. She wasn't a petite woman who could easily sit on a man's lap, but Mitch wouldn't let her go.

"If you want I could get another chair," he said. "But I like you right here."

"Or I can sit on the bed."

"Is that what you want?"

She almost said yes. But it wasn't true. Couldn't she, just once, stop all the thinking and analyzing and let go? Even if it was just this, only this…She shook her head.

"Good." He swung his legs so that they were both facing the monitor, but with his hand rubbing her back, if he thought she was going to pay attention to what was happening on the screen he was sadly mistaken. "Comfortable?"

"Yes, but I have to be crushing you."

"Right." He moved his hand, and she immediately grieved the loss, but it was back, only under her shirt this time.

She felt her nipples tighten and peak under her skimpy bra and thin cotton T-shirt. Sliding him a sidelong glance, she saw that his eyes were on the monitor. His hands were another story. The one stroking her back had stopped at the closure of her bra. In a matter of seconds he worked the clasp free. She stiffened, and he kissed the side of her neck.

Though anxious over what he'd do next, she forced

herself to relax. He splayed his hand at her waist and across her ribs until his fingers grazed the underside of her left breast. She swallowed a whimper as his hand moved under the loosened bra and touched her nipple.

She squirmed against him, amazed at the swelling thickness beneath her fanny. How had she not felt him getting so hard? He'd distracted her, that's how. He was still distracting her. She jerked when he pinched her nipple.

"I need to taste you," he whispered.

"But the—" She stopped speaking and drew a shaky breath. They were sitting right here in front of the monitors. They'd pay attention, right? Nothing would happen anyway. Except maybe she'd burst if she didn't feel his mouth on her soon.

They both reached for the hem of her shirt at the same time. He yanked it up first, and she finished the job. Her bra practically took care of itself and landed somewhere near her feet.

She heard his sharp intake of breath as his gaze traveled over her exposed breasts. His tongue drew across his lower lip and he muttered a quiet curse that might have been offensive another time. But not now. Not when he was looking at her as if he'd never seen anything more desirable in his life.

A rush of pure pleasure surged through her veins and pooled in a flood of warmth between her thighs. He reverently touched the crown of one breast and then the other, the slight tremor in his hands so endearingly sweet her heart lurched.

The warmth of his breath bathing her skin was almost more than she could stand, and she closed her eyes, willing him to put his mouth on her.

"Ah, Kate, when did you grow up to be so beautiful?" He nuzzled the skin near her collarbone, trailed the tip of his tongue to the valley between her breasts.

She arched her back, silently telling him what she wanted, her insides quaking so badly he had to feel her need.

He cradled the weight of one breast with his palm and gazed at her with a longing in his eyes that stole her breath. "Tell me what you want," he whispered.

She cupped her other breast, lightly pinching her aching nipple, and lifted it toward his mouth. Her boldness unnerved her, but one look at the fierce desire in his face erased all shyness.

He lowered his head and used his mouth with a hunger that shook her to her core.

14

MITCH HADN'T TRULY KNOWN how much he wanted this until now. How much he needed to feel his arms around Kate's slender yielding body, feel the strong rhythm of her steady heartbeat against his chest. He wanted to bury himself inside her sweet softness. He'd be a liar to deny otherwise, but what he felt was so much more than the need for physical release. He didn't know when the switch had flipped in his mind. Had it been when he'd seen her standing at the kitchen door that first night? Katie, all grown-up and filled out in ways he couldn't have imagined back in the day. But that was just the physical aspect. He was a normal guy. He reacted to beautiful women. He'd slept with more than his share. But with Kate, it was the way she didn't care that her ponytail was crooked. How she walked in her worn boots. He liked that she left empty iced tea glasses all over the house, then blamed him for it. That when she laughed hard, she kinda snorted. And this.

Forcing himself to take it slow, he tasted the crown of one firm mound, leisurely rolling his tongue over her pearled nipple, pleased when she moaned low in her throat. He loved her breasts, the shape, the color of her nipples, the creamy texture. They couldn't be more perfect, as if they were meant for him alone.

He flicked the tip of his tongue over the tight nub, and then circled it. "I hope you're keeping an eye on the monitors since I'm too busy," he murmured against her silky skin.

"You're evil."

"I could stop."

"Do not underestimate my ability to hurt you."

He smiled, and ministered to her other breast, unsure how long he could take this self-inflicted punishment. Underneath her sweet little fanny, he was so hard an explosion wasn't out of the question. He switched from gentle laving to suckling her hard, and when she made that sexy throaty sound again, every part of him went on full alert. He struggled for a self-control that rarely failed him, and barely cared that he was losing the battle.

"Mitch." Kate framed his face with her hands and urged him to lift his head. "Mitch, wait."

Grudgingly he looked up, confused over whether he'd actually heard her speak, or if it had been the blood roaring in his ears.

"I have to tell you—" Her breathing came in short ragged pants, her green eyes darker than he'd ever seen them. "The monitors—I can't watch them when you—" She visibly swallowed. "When you do those things."

"What things?" He smiled, inhaling her sweet feminine scent.

"Stop it."

"Stop what?"

"Your breath…it tickles."

"You want me to stop breathing?"

She jabbed him with her elbow.

Grunting, he slid both arms around her, imprisoning

her while he kneaded her bare breasts. "You're perfect. I want to look at you, but I don't want you to get up."

"I have to. Someone could've stolen every last heifer in the past few minutes and I wouldn't have known. Oh." She arched into his hands, her nipples rock-hard against his palms, her entire body trembling.

The vibration did nothing to relieve the throbbing in his cock. She was right. They should cool it. The sun would start to come up soon and there would be no worries until tonight. Then they'd have the rest of the day. But she was so warm and ready, and if he were to slip his hand between her thighs he knew she'd be wet for him. "Here. Angle back toward the monitors, but don't worry about watching them. I'll watch the monitors."

He gently urged her to swing her legs toward the monitor, clenching his teeth at the seductive pressure of her backside on his cock.

"But I still—" She started when he jerked down the tab of her zipper. "What are you doing?"

"Relax, lean back against my chest," he whispered and kissed the side of her neck. "Close your eyes if you want. I've got the monitors." He slid his hand inside the waistband of her shorts, found the elastic of her panties, felt her renewed trembling. "I've got you."

KATE TOOK A DEEP BREATH.

"Are you okay?" He moved his hand, silently asking her to loosen up.

She wasn't trying to shut him out. He'd startled her, and the reaction had been pure reflex.

Slowly, lightly, he stroked the soft skin of her inner thigh. With his other hand, he found her left breast and rubbed her still-erect nipple. The brief distraction was all he'd needed to push aside the crotch of her panties and slide his fingers into her damp folds.

The sudden avalanche of sensual excitement was almost too much for Kate. His mouth on her neck, one hand on her breast, thumbing her nipple, two fingers of his other hand probing and deft as they entered her. She couldn't help but tense, but showing no mercy, he slid deeper inside until she whimpered.

Squirming didn't help. The friction on her clit almost sent her over the edge. She clutched his forearm and pushed back against his chest. The movement only improved his access. His fingers retreated and then re-entered, swift and hard, while his thumb rubbed her clit.

"Oh, Mitch." She was going to come too fast. Without him. This wasn't how it was supposed to be….

"Shh, sweetheart, let go."

She resisted. It wasn't fair. She wanted to see his face. She wanted to kiss him. Touch him. Give him pleasure, too.

"I love that you're so slick and wet," he whispered. "Come for me." He slowly circled his thumb over her clit, then faster, mimicking the motion on her nipple.

"Oh, no." She dug her nails into his arm. "Oh, Mitch."

"Come on, Kate." His voice was so raspy he sounded as if he might come, too.

Knowing he was that turned on was all it took. An overwhelming heat swept over her, and the spasms started, shuddering through her, around her, until her need for release was so great an unexpected cry rose from her throat and shattered the darkness.

Her entire body convulsed and still he wouldn't ease

the pressure of his fingers between her thighs. Just when she thought she couldn't take any more, another wave crashed over her, sending a fresh burst of sensation spiraling through her, starting at her core and tingling through her limbs. She went rigid, and then limp in his arms.

Mitch muttered something. It could have been a curse—she was too incoherent to be sure. He set her on her feet, and kicked away the chair. Then he picked her up and carried her the short distance to the bed. Still weak, she fell inelegantly against the pillows, and watched him strip off his shirt.

The sight of his sleekly muscled chest and shoulders ignited another fire in her belly. When he unsnapped his jeans and pushed them down his lean hips, her chest painfully constricted. He got rid of the dark blue boxers, and then he was all muscle and thick swollen sex.

The languidness she'd just felt, vanished, replaced with an excitement that thrummed through her veins. He reached for her shorts, and she lifted her bottom while he slid them from her body. Her bikini panties followed, and then he stood back, gazing at her nakedness, his face no longer unreadable. His eyes glittered with an intensity that was almost frightening, making him look as though he could devour her whole.

She moved over to make room for him on the small bed. "What about a condom?"

This time there was no mistaking the curse he muttered in earnest, before he turned and searched the floor, affording her a heart-stopping view of his perfect ass. He retrieved the jeans he'd discarded and dug into his pocket.

Something flickered on the monitors, drawing her

gaze. But it was nothing, and at this point, she wasn't sure she would've cared.

He followed her gaze, but ignored the screen and crawled in beside her. "I can't wait," he whispered hoarsely.

The admission washed over her like a heat wave. "It's close enough to daybreak, anyway."

In spite of everything going on, all he wanted was her. The idea sent a shiver of pleasure down her spine, and she blindly reached for him, gingerly touching the crown and then drawing her finger down his hard silky length. His penis pulsed and jerked upward.

Oh, how she wanted to explore some more, but with lightning swiftness he moved her hand and sheathed himself. He wasted no time easing her legs apart and positioning himself between them. He paused long enough to study the secret he'd uncovered, lightly running his finger over her clit, before lifting her legs up to his shoulders and then guiding himself to her opening.

"I promise we'll take it slow later," he said, his eyes drifting closed as he pushed inside of her.

She jumped at the invasion, not because it was unpleasant, just startling. He was a big man in every way, and she was relieved that he took it slow enough for her to get used to him.

"You okay?" he asked, brushing the hair away from her face.

She nodded, and flattened her palms against his chest, enjoying the feel of muscles that bunched and relaxed with his every movement. "It feels good. You feel good."

"Oh, sweetheart, you have no idea." He slid in

deeper, and she instinctively tried to lift her hips, but with her legs already hooked over his shoulders, she couldn't go anywhere.

He pushed in all the way, and she nearly flew off the mattress. He promptly eased back.

"No, it's okay," she assured him, but then saw the real reason for his retreat.

He stared down at where their bodies joined, and then spread her lips and touched her. Right there, and this time she did come off the mattress.

He moaned low in his throat. "That's right, baby," he whispered, and found her left breast, kneading, pinching, teasing. "Come for me again."

"No, you," she panted. "It's your turn."

His mouth curved. "Oh, I'm gonna come with you."

Increasing the pressure on her clit, he circled her nipple and drove himself into her. She met every thrust, then convulsed, crying out with pleasure. He erupted a moment later, trembling against her, the primal moan coming from him almost otherworldly. He took her legs off his shoulders and then collapsed next to her.

"Wow!" Kate pressed her lips together. Had she said that out loud?

"I agree," he whispered, his breath warming her skin where he kissed the side of her neck. "You're amazing."

She laughed softly. "No, *you're* amazing."

"Hmm…" Mitch lightly bit her earlobe. "You want to waste time arguing?"

"Unless you have something else in mind." At the pleasant exploration of his lips and teeth, she closed her eyes, and arched slightly, her overly sensitive body beginning to respond again.

The curve of his smile rasped against her skin, and he splayed his big hand across her belly.

"I can't believe it," she murmured, tensing when his fingers stretched toward the juncture of her thighs. "This is too surreal."

"What?"

"You, me, here. Like this."

He chuckled softly. "If you want me to stop…" His clever hand made a mockery of his words as he slid between her thighs. He covered her mouth with his and swallowed her moan.

"NO, YOU DON'T." Kate scooted out of his reach. "You're not allowed to even look at me."

Chuckling, Mitch had followed her out of the bedroom while he pulled on a T-shirt. His feet were still bare, so were hers. It was already ten-thirty and neither of them had even had their first cup of coffee yet. "For how long?"

"A week."

"The hell you say."

"Okay, twenty-four hours." She hurried down the stairs, groaning and rubbing her bottom. "Just so you know, that's being generous because there's no way I'll have recovered by then."

He stood at the top and watched her disappear into the kitchen, admiring her shiny freshly washed hair. "I'll give you until seven tonight," he called, grinning when he heard her fake howl of exasperation. The truth was, he hadn't recovered yet himself. Going three rounds in six hours had damn near killed him. But he'd get over it.

While she started the coffee, he returned to the room

and fished out a clean pair of socks. Out of habit, he glanced out the window at the cattle grazing in the distance. Thankfully, they were still there. He hadn't thought there'd be a problem after they'd abandoned the monitors, but then again, he hadn't been thinking all that much.

Making love with Kate had been amazing. *She* was amazing. It wasn't just the sex. That had been monumental, but something else had happened. Something deep inside had shifted, almost as if a part of him had been broken and now it was fixed. Only he couldn't figure out what was wrong in the first place. He liked his job. He liked living in Palm Beach. He had a pretty damn good life. Nothing needed fixing.

He hoped things stayed that way. With Kate. If he saw a single trace of regret in her eyes, it would kill him. Bad enough he had his own conscience to deal with. He'd sworn he wouldn't take advantage of her after her breakup, swore to himself and to her. He could rationalize that she'd come after him, pushed him hard by waving Brad in his face, harassed him with those skimpy dresses. But none of those things changed the truth. Mitch was a damn hypocrite.

He was borrowing trouble, as his mother would say. No sense ruining the morning. It was done. If there were pieces to pick up later, he'd man up. Yeah, because he'd made such a good job of it so far.

He pushed the curtains farther apart so that he could see beyond the stables that had once housed a dozen horses. The grass was still pretty green, but only because it was early July and the underground spring that ran through the property hadn't yet dried up for the summer.

Already he could see patches of yellow from the heat and lack of water. By next month the landscape would look like a hay field. Unless he got his ass out there and finished repairing the irrigation system.

But that would be a waste of time. He wouldn't be here that long, and even if he caught the rustlers, there was no guarantee his parents would return soon to work the ranch. Truth was, he wasn't a hundred percent certain they would ever come back. But then, they hadn't believed him when he'd said he would stop the rustlers. They'd just done what they always did. Placate him and move on with their lives.

It disturbed the hell out of him to think the land could remain vacant, maybe sold. Especially after having been home for the past ten days.

Funny, how he still considered the place home. He hadn't actually been involved in the ranch for over a decade, and had no idea what worked and what didn't. Some of the equipment had been sold off, but the tractor remained in the barn, as well as two quads and most of the tack. Mitch remembered the day three years ago when he'd teased his father about switching from a horse to a quad for rounding up the cattle. His dad had laughed indignantly, but then admitted he was getting too old to cover the spread.

There had been no hidden accusation in his voice or face. He'd always respected his son's desire to strike out on his own, but for the first time, Mitch had felt the stab of guilt. In those days there had still been help, three cowhands, two who'd been with the Colters for over twenty years. But that hadn't mattered, at least it hadn't lessened Mitch's guilt. Not enough to get him to return.

In fact, to his shame, in trying to avoid the guilt, his visits home had dwindled.

"Hey, you."

He heard Kate's voice coming from downstairs, and he grabbed his boots and took them with him.

Standing near the bottom step, she had one hand on her hip, in her other she held a mug. "If you want coffee, I suggest you get your tail down here because I'm not climbing up there again."

"Here I was waiting for you to serve me in bed."

She smiled sweetly. "Ever have caffeine withdrawal?"

"Man, you're grumpy when you don't get enough sleep," he grumbled, catching her around the waist as he left the stairs.

She gasped, holding the mug away from her body. "If you spill this coffee—"

He kissed her, taking advantage of her open mouth and slipping his tongue between her lips. She tasted of sugar and cream and strong French roast. Her warm soft body nestled against him, she felt like heaven. "Morning," he murmured against her mouth.

She sighed. "Don't think you're going to sweet-talk me into—"

The slam of a car door had them straightening and drawing apart. Their startled eyes met briefly, and then she followed him to the front window. He didn't open the curtains, only pushed one side back far enough for him to see but not be seen.

He exhaled harshly when he spotted their visitor. "What the hell does he want?"

"Who is it?"

"That Realtor."

Kate looked down at Mitch's stockinged feet. "Better put your boots on," she said and slipped on the pair of sandals she'd left near the door.

He watched with growing irritation as the man came up the walk. "I'm not answering the door."

"But he sees your truck."

"So? That should give him a hint that he's not wanted."

She laid a hand on his arm. "If you don't answer, he'll probably just come back."

Mitch knew she was right, and privately acknowledged the disproportionate anger he felt toward the man, but that didn't stop him from wanting to throw the guy off the property on his ass. He pulled on his boots while he waited for the second knock, and then went to open the door.

The man had been scanning the pasture but abruptly turned when the door opened. "Howdy, you remember me, don't ya? Levi Dodd," he said to Mitch, and then removed his Stetson when he saw Kate, and nodded to her. "Sure is another scorcher." He withdrew a linen handkerchief and mopped his sweaty forehead.

"What can I do for you?" Mitch asked, unsmiling, and folding his arms across his chest.

Kate secretly elbowed him. She probably thought he should invite the guy inside. Tough. He wasn't going to do it. She moved closer, her soft plump breast hitting the back of his arm.

"Come in, Dodd," Mitch said grudgingly, and gave her a frustrated look as he stepped back to let the Realtor inside.

She smiled. "We were just having coffee," she said to the man. "May I get you a cup?"

"No, ma'am, but thanks for asking." He surveyed the

pale yellow painted walls and oak floors, his gaze lingering on the hand-carved banister. "Nice place. Your folks did real well maintaining the old house. What year was it built?"

Mitch really wished Kate had gone to the kitchen so he wouldn't have to suffer her disapproving look when he reamed the guy's ass. "It's still not for sale, Mr. Dodd. For your sake, I hope you had another reason for coming out this far."

The Realtor's face flushed, and Mitch got the impression it wasn't from the heat but anger. "I appreciate your reluctance, Mitch. Believe me, I do understand." He pressed his thin lips together and gave his head a slow shake of regret. "I hope you understand why I'm gonna have to give your father a call. After all, he is the rightful owner. And this place can only lay fallow for so long and not depreciate. That few head of cattle you brought in can't mean much."

Rage boiled inside of Mitch. He refused to look at Kate. "Do what you have to do, but right now, you need to leave."

The man seemed surprised, and then a dark look passed briefly over his face. He stuffed his handkerchief into his pocket and unhurriedly resettled the tan Stetson on his head. The cocky lift of his mouth didn't gel with the good ole boy facade. "Y'all have a nice day."

Mitch waited until the man was outside before he slammed the door. "Son of a bitch."

"I know it's hard to hear." Kate put an arm around his waist. "I wanted to strangle him last week for even asking about the Sugarloaf. But if the place is too much for your parents," she said gently, "you have to consider that the money they could get for it might be more important to them."

"I have money if they need it. I've invested well."

"Someone still has to run the ranch."

His heart raced like a Thoroughbred. "I could do it."

She drew back, regarding him with wide, shocked eyes. "What do you mean?"

Hell, he didn't know what he meant. He was getting ahead of himself. Stalking away from her prying eyes, he rammed a hand through his damp hair.

"Mitch, what do you mean?" she repeated.

He couldn't answer.

15

A WEEK AFTER THEY'D MADE LOVE for the first time, Kate decided that learning patience was her lesson in this whole thing with Mitch. She had to believe that, or else she'd hog-tie him and refuse to cut him loose until he answered every one of her questions. She didn't have many. One in particular burned hotly in her mind. What was his long-term plan for returning home?

If she thought she'd get a straight answer, she'd probably say to hell with patience and ask again. But he obviously wasn't ready to have that talk, and frankly, she wasn't sure she was, either. The idea of Mitch moving back to West Texas was more than she could process. It didn't seem to matter that, deep down, she knew the likelihood of his returning was slim. Whether he'd admit it or not, it was possible that he was romanticizing the notion of coming back to take up the reins, an emotional knee jerk to the prospect of his parents selling the land. Ironic, really, since he was so concerned about his relationship with her being based on a rebound.

The grim reality of the daily ranch work versus his glamorous life would be a jolt. Apparently he'd forgotten that he'd left for a reason. It didn't matter that he'd been brought up on a ranch. He wasn't cowboy material. He'd never made any bones about that.

Sadly, that was something she herself should have remembered. Too late, now that she knew she was in love with him. What a mess. She thought her childish crush had been only that, but she was wrong. Horribly wrong. In her defense, as a kid herself she'd fallen for a boy, but now, Mitch the man was so much better than she could've dreamed.

Sighing, she returned their washed breakfast dishes to the cabinet, careful of the loose middle shelf. Mitch hadn't gotten to the kitchen repairs yet, he'd been too busy servicing the outside equipment. She'd done what she could inside, but she wasn't very handy so she stuck to simple tasks and ran errands to town when necessary.

The domesticity they'd settled into was far too comfortable and a bit scary. Mornings were for chores, in the afternoon they napped, and as the sun sank to the horizon they made love. Taking shifts to watch the monitors had become a joke. They spent the entire time talking or making out like two high school kids. Right before dawn they'd crawl into bed and make love again. Man, she was going to miss this.

All that thinking about Mitch's future had forced her to think of her own. She still hadn't spoken to Dennis, even though he continued to call on a daily basis. She also hadn't decided whether she was going to go back and teach at the end of summer. Part of her wanted to leave West Texas behind in a cloud of dust. Just strike out and see a world she'd always dreamed of. But if Mitch stayed…

God, it was all too difficult to contemplate, let alone

make a decision about. The only thing she knew she had to do was call Dennis and close that door once and for all.

She got her phone out of her purse and flipped it open. No time like the present, especially when she saw he'd left yet another message.

She pressed his speed dial number, vowing to erase it the second this was finished.

"Kate? Is that really you?"

His voice alone was enough to get her angry all over again. "It is."

"I've been doing everything I could think of to get in touch with you. To explain."

"Everything but look me in the face," she said, her voice as steely as Mitch's eyes. "As for an explanation, don't bother."

"But—"

"Dennis, I don't care. In fact, you did me a favor. Now I'll do you one. Don't call me again. I mean it. It's over and I have nothing left in me that cares to speak to you. Am I being clear?"

He didn't respond, at least not for about twenty seconds. "I just wanted to—"

She hung up her phone, a new lightness making her take actual delight in deleting his number from her list. To think she'd ever believed she'd been in love with that ass. Even if Mitch left tomorrow, she'd be grateful that he'd showed her what it was to truly want someone. And be wanted.

She heard an engine and her gaze snapped to the wall clock as she hurried to the window. It was Mitch. He had left two hours ago, after sharing that he had a surprise for her. She tore out of the house and met him as he got out of the truck, not his truck, but the old clunker the Colters used around the ranch for dropping hay.

"Well, where's my surprise?"

He grinned. "Get in, and I'll show you."

Confused, she glanced in the truck's rusty old bed as she climbed into the passenger side. "I thought you went to get it."

"I did." He'd left the truck running, and he promptly reversed and turned them around.

"Where's your truck?"

"Too many questions."

"This is cruel and unusual punishment," she said, throwing him a quick glare before scanning the landscape on either side of the driveway. Earlier she'd suspected he'd gone to pick up a horse, but he wasn't towing a trailer so what the heck had he been doing for three hours? "Where are we going?"

"You'll see in a few minutes." He reached over and slipped his hand around the back of her neck and tried to draw her across the bench seat.

She playfully bit his arm, and he yelped. "Don't be a baby. I barely touched—" Something shiny caught her eye. She squinted toward the McGregors' ranch at the reflection of sun hitting metal. There were at least three hundred vacant acres between the Colters' land and where the McGregors' house stood, so she couldn't imagine what was out there. "Do you see that?"

"What?" His obvious attempt to sound innocent drew a sharp look from her.

"Come on," she said, and then realized they were headed straight for the object in question. Her eyes stayed trained on the area and within a minute she saw the small white single engine with a red stripe sitting on a stretch of dirt road. "That's a plane."

Mitch laughed. "Yes, it is."

"Where did you get it?"

"I rented it."

"From where?"

He shrugged. "I know a guy who knows a guy."

"Seriously. Where did it come from?"

"I drove to Houston and flew it back. A friend hooked me up with a charter service. This is an older model, so I got a good deal on it for two days use."

He parked the truck a short distance away, and Kate jumped out. She'd never flown in a plane that small before, and she was torn between excitement and a modicum of fear. "You said this is an older model?"

He came up behind her, hugged her against his chest and kissed the top of her head. "You don't trust me?" he asked with a smile in his voice.

She turned around in his arms and kissed him briefly on the mouth. "When are we going up?"

"I was going to say now, but if you have something else in mind—"

She gave him a playful shove. He'd already started getting hard, making her heart pound. "You're incorrigible," she scolded. Never in her life had she felt more desirable than when she was with Mitch. It seemed as if he literally couldn't keep his hands off her. The way he acted, you'd think she was the world's most celebrated supermodel. If he were to stay, would he always feel that way about her?

Oh, she had to stop going there. What were the chances

he would stay and be happy with the daily grind of ranch life? Playing what-if was only going to make her crazy.

"Let's go," he said. "We'll scout out a place where we can have a picnic tomorrow. Ah, that reminds me." He got a bag out of the truck and stowed it in some netting in the back of the plane.

"What is that?"

"Enough with the questions," he said, grinning when she glared, and helped her into the burgundy-colored leather copilot's seat.

She buckled herself in and looked around while he walked to the other side of the plane. The inside was immaculate, comfortable and very spiffy with a carpeted floor. Behind her was a bench seat with individual backs where two people could easily fit.

Once he'd settled into the pilot's seat and buckled himself in, he put on headphones and motioned for her to do the same with the extra set.

"It's easier to talk with these on," he explained as he flipped switches with serious concentration.

He turned on the engine, frowning when it took a moment to catch.

"Everything okay?" she asked nervously.

"What?" He glanced over at her. "Yeah, I just forgot something."

"To do with the plane?"

"No, sunglasses for you." He flipped down a visor in front of her face. "The sun is in back of us, so it shouldn't be too bad."

The propeller on the nose began to spin, speeding up until it was just a blur.

"Ready?"

She nodded, and not until he patted her hand did she notice her white-knuckle grip on the armrest. She relaxed, gave him a wry smile, and he winked before slipping on a pair of aviator-style dark glasses and then returning his full attention to getting them off the ground.

They were airborne before she knew it, ascending into the clear blue sky, the expanse of pastureland falling away. Amazingly, she started to loosen up. She'd never been afraid to fly, and in fact, often enjoyed it. It was just that she'd never flown in such an itty-bitty plane before. But Mitch clearly knew what he was doing, and as her confidence grew, so did her delight as they soared over the glistening stream where she liked to water Lil when she rode the mare in the afternoons.

"Look over there." Mitch's voice came through the headphones, and she turned to see him pointing to the left. "Part of your land, right?"

Kate shifted to see where he meant, and then nodded. Thanks to an underground spring, the emerald-green patch of grass and trees and shallow pool was like an oasis in the middle of nowhere. "I haven't been out there in a while. Too far a ride when it's this hot."

"After we circle, I'll see if there's a place to land nearby. Tomorrow we can picnic there."

She started to remind him that there were two other similar spots on the Sugarloaf, but closer to the house. Quickly she stopped herself, excited just thinking about all the privacy they would have way out here.

He reached for her hand and brought it to his lips. "Or maybe we shouldn't wait until tomorrow."

"We don't have a picnic."

A sly grin curved his mouth. "I'll make do."

She blushed, thinking about their early-morning marathon. "Save your strength, flyboy."

Mitch chuckled, and returned his hand to the controls. "This is great, isn't it? Being way up here. There's nothing else like it."

"It's pretty cool, I have to admit."

They flew for the better part of an hour, over the McGregors' land, the Double R and the Sugarloaf. He pointed out landmarks she didn't recognize from the air, and described how incredible it was to fly at sunset over the Caribbean, the rush of dipping toward the Grand Canyon and coasting over Yellowstone Park. He told her about the other places still on his list.

Watching him made her smile. It also made her a bit sad. He was certainly in his element. There was an excitement in his face and voice that reminded her of the old Mitch, the boy she'd known half a lifetime ago. But the more she heard him talk, the more she saw the animation take over his features, the more she realized that Mitch was never coming back to be a rancher.

The knowledge hurt, even though she somehow had known the answer to that question all along. She was a fool to have hoped even for a second. He didn't belong here anymore, and she was going to have to hold her head up while he walked away.

She felt a definite shift in their flight pattern and clutched the armrest. "Is something wrong?"

"Nope. We're circling back."

"Home?"

He shook his head, his mouth curving in an enigmatic smile.

EXCITEMENT STIRRED Mitch's blood. Not only because of the wicked things he had in mind for Kate. But seeing all that unused land surrounding his parents' spread gave him hope. He knew the McGregors and the Reynolds quite well; their kids were slightly ahead of him in school. They were nice people, who probably had no desire to leave the land they'd grown up on, but he suspected they wouldn't mind selling off a few parcels. Enough to allow him to expand if he chose to stay and reclaim his family's ranch.

He brought the plane down as close to the small grove of trees as was safely possible. He could tell the descent had made Kate nervous, but she hadn't said a word. Flying in a plane this small took some getting used to. A few more times up and she'd be okay.

After he helped her to the ground, he got out the small bag he'd stowed. In it he had bottled water and a blanket. They found a flat grassy area behind the privacy of the trees, and he shook out the blanket.

As soon as Kate saw it, she laughed. "You sneaky devil."

"Come here."

She stopped at the edge of the blanket and folded her arms across her chest. "I thought we were having our picnic tomorrow."

He caught her wrist, ignoring her surprised gasp when he pulled her arms apart and forced them to her side. "I'm having mine now," he murmured, and yanked up the hem of her knit top.

She automatically lifted her arms, and he drew the shirt over her head and tossed it into the tall grass. Her bra had a front closure, which he easily unfastened. He pushed aside the cups and bared her breasts.

"You are so damn beautiful," he whispered before dipping his head and drawing an already hardened nipple into his mouth.

She tugged at his T-shirt with impatient jerks, but he made her wait while he slid the bra straps off her shoulders and let the wisp of silk fall to the ground.

"If someone catches us, I'll just die," she said, but that didn't stop her from nearly ripping the T-shirt off his body.

"There's no one around for miles. I checked before we landed." He lightly stroked his thumb down her cheek, hoping like hell he could restrain himself long enough for some foreplay. Stopping here had been unintended. He truly had planned on waiting for a picnic tomorrow. But she'd looked so damn beautiful sitting in the copilot's seat, the sun shining in her hair and painting her skin a warm gold. "Lie down, sweetheart."

She surprised him by lowering her head and nipping at his erect nipple. He jerked, and she bit him, stoking the savage intensity with which he wanted her. The sudden desire to pin her to the blanket and push his cock into her literally weakened his knees.

"You have any idea how much trouble you're asking for," he murmured, gripping her upper arms in a plea for her to stop.

She lifted her head long enough for him to see the mischievous tilt of her lips. "Nothing more than I can handle."

"You think so?" He smiled, and forced her back a step.

Her eyes widened a fraction, and then so did her smile. "Bring it on."

He claimed her mouth and urged her down until they

were both on their knees. She gasped softly when he pushed her back against the blanket, holding her down with his kiss and one hand kneading her breast, while he rid her of her shorts and panties. Once she was completely naked, he drew back to look at her. She was so amazing it was a miracle he'd managed an ounce of restraint.

"Your jeans," she said, reaching blindly. "Take them off."

He ignored her and spread her thighs apart.

She tensed, but only for a moment, and then watched as he rolled his tongue over one fully blossomed pink nipple. He didn't trust himself to take off his jeans yet. There was too much he wanted to do with her and he'd already proven he couldn't trust himself when it came to Kate.

He suckled her for a while and then laved the other nipple.

She squirmed when he trailed the tip of his tongue to her navel, and then wedged himself between her thighs. He stretched out on his belly, nipping and teasing with his tongue until he'd gently spread her fleshy lips. She jerked, her backside coming off the blanket. He took advantage of the opportunity and flattened his tongue against her, licking slowly, finding the nub, tasting her wet heat and dangerously fueling his own arousal.

"I hope you brought a—oh." She was cut off by a whimper, her hands fisting the blanket on either side of her body.

Hell. A condom. How could he have been so stupid? Maybe he still had one in his jeans' pocket. It didn't matter. She was close to coming. Ah, how much he wanted to please her.

"Mitch, I can't—you have to stop."

He went full throttle, flicking his tongue over her clit, using just the right amount of pressure he knew she liked. He used his forefinger to enter her, but he'd hardly pushed in when she moaned loudly and bucked against his mouth. As much as he wanted to be inside of her, this was good, too.

He stayed with her, even when she curled up and grabbed a handful of his hair, and nearly scalped him. He finally retreated, when she started to still and pleaded with him to stop.

She was still breathing hard when he drew himself up to stretch out beside her. "You're going to be the death of me," she said between pants.

"But what a way to go." Grinning, he stroked a breast and lightly kissed the crown.

"You still have your jeans on."

"I forgot the condoms."

She turned on her side, cupped his arousal over his fly and deliberately moistened her lips. "That doesn't have to be a problem, as you've already demonstrated."

Mitch smiled and kissed her, slow and deep. He'd never been a selfish lover, not that he was a saint. But it was different with Kate. He drew back and touched her cheek. "Let's get back up in the air."

She looked startled, confused. "Now?"

He nodded. "I swear I hadn't planned this. I really did want to bring a picnic tomorrow, then have you for dessert."

She punched his arm.

"Ouch." He chuckled. "Are you complaining?"

A shy smile tugged at her lips. "I'm not that stupid. It's just that—"

"Come on." He grabbed her hand and pulled her up with him before he changed his mind, which he was too close to doing. So far they'd flown north by northwest, and there was still quite a bit of ground he wanted to cover before returning to the ranch.

He helped gather her clothes, and then slid on his shirt while trying hard to keep his gaze off her naked body. As she got dressed, he folded the blanket, and then circled the plane for a quick check of the tires and propeller. Within minutes, they were headed down the grassy runway.

"I could get used to this," Kate said once the wheels left the ground and they lifted off.

Mitch glanced over at her, and smiled. She had her visor down, her head back, eyes half-closed "You were nervous earlier."

"Only because I hadn't ridden in a small plane before."

"Pretty awesome, huh?"

Her expression turned oddly wistful. "I can see why you love it so much."

"Best thing I ever did was get my pilot's license. There's nothing like flying." He reached over to give her thigh a squeeze. "You good for another hour or two?"

"Sure. Where are we going?"

"East. Toward the Kingston Ranch."

"I don't think there's much happening over there. Maybe you hadn't heard, but George passed away two years ago."

"I heard. And though it's not my first choice, I was hoping Ida might be willing to sell me a hundred acres."

Kate straightened. Out of the corner of his eye he saw her turn to stare at him. "Why?"

Maybe he was being a fool, but he wanted to gauge how she'd feel about him returning for good. Not that he'd made the decision for certain. But then that's what made him a fool. He kept his gaze on the terrain. "In order to compete in today's market, I'd have to expand, triple the original herd, hire more men, modernize, specialize." He paused. "Figure out how prepared I am to dive in."

"Are you?" she asked thinly. "Prepared to come back?"

"That's something we need to discuss," he said slowly, and finally looked at her. But movement on the ground diverted his attention. He squinted at the dark green Jeep sitting in the middle of nowhere, the man getting out. "Who the hell is that?"

Kate followed his gaze; at the same time an ATV shot out of a cluster of mesquite. "It almost looks like the sheriff. The one on the ATV, I don't know." She pointed north. "Look."

Two more men approached on horseback, greeted by the man on the ATV. Mitch dropped lower, drawing the attention of the four men. Quickly he tipped the nose of the plane back upward to preserve his and Kate's identity. But not before he recognized the ATV rider. It was Brad. So why the hell was he meeting the sheriff out in the middle of nowhere?

16

IF MITCH HAD MEANT TO confuse her, turn her mind to complete mush, he'd done a bang-up job. First, he'd had her convinced he could never love anything as much as he did flying, and then he did a complete turnaround, suggesting he might want to return to ranching. Had he only said that because he thought that's what she wanted to hear? Did he think her so fragile that sex had changed her expectations, her needs?

The truth was, sadly, it had. Her needs, anyway. She wanted him now more than ever. But he didn't know that. She'd made no demands, hadn't expressed how she felt, so he had no business coddling her. Making assumptions. Offering her false hope, because, damn it, yes, she did want him to come back. But she'd die before she'd admit that to him.

They'd flown directly back to the ranch, largely in silence. Mitch was obviously preoccupied with the covert meeting between the sheriff and Brad. Even though she hadn't truly considered going out with him, Kate hated that Brad might be mixed up in the rustling, oddly, even more than she disliked the idea that the sheriff could be involved. But she and Mitch agreed that the out-of-the-way meeting between Brad and the sheriff made no sense. And who were the other mystery men?

"I should go out with Brad," she said as soon as they were in the truck, headed to the house. "See what I can find out."

A frown etched deep creases between his brows as Mitch turned to stare at her in disbelief.

"Look out." She clutched the edge of the seat as he swerved to miss a clump of cactus.

He righted the truck. "I hope you're not serious because the answer is no."

"Number one, it's a good idea, and number two, I didn't ask for your permission."

"Come on, be sensible." He sounded annoyed. "Brad's not going to give you squat. If he's involved, he only asked you out because he wants information from you."

Kate lifted her chin, dying to say something, but no witty retort came to her. His remark had hurt. Okay, she was no raving beauty, but was it so hard to believe that Brad might have asked her out simply because he was interested?

"Hey, I didn't mean that the way it sounded," Mitch said after a moment.

"Oh, how did it sound?"

"Kate, I'm sorry. No excuse, but I'm wound up." He reached for her hand, and she let him take it and bring it to his lips for a brief kiss.

They drove the couple of minutes it took to get home. Again there was mostly silence. Mitch seemed wrapped up in his own thoughts and blessedly dropped the subject of Brad. Kate couldn't stop thinking about how Mitch looked while they were flying. He'd belonged up there. Anyone could've seen how much being a pilot was a part of who he was.

Feeling absurdly claustrophobic, she could barely wait for the truck to stop before she opened her door and jumped out. Mitch was right behind her, oblivious to her deteriorating mood. He'd extended his apology and thought all was well. She'd let him believe that.

"I'm going to do something I should've done two weeks ago," he said, pocketing his keys and digging out his cell phone. "Find out just who the hell that sheriff is. I'm sure the county commissioners did their due diligence before the election, but that doesn't mean he isn't crooked."

"You're right, and of course I'll help—" she cleared her throat "—when I get back." They'd made it to the porch and she avoided his gaze while he opened the door for her. "I haven't been home in days and I need to pick up a few things." What she really wanted was to spend the night in her own bed, alone, with time to think, but it wasn't fair to leave him to watch the monitors until dawn.

"Sure." He studied her face. "Take your time."

"I can bring back dinner if you like, although I may not make it until near dark."

Concern darkening his eyes, he pulled her close. "Is everything okay?"

She nodded. "I'm just tired."

"Maybe you should stay at the Sugarloaf tonight." He brushed the hair away from her cheek, the tenderness in his face making her want to weep. "I'd miss you, but at least you'd get some rest."

"But then you wouldn't get any relief from surveil-lance."

He snorted. "We gave up taking shifts a week ago."

"True."

He looked as if he didn't really want her to go, yet he gave her a quick kiss and then turned her determinedly toward her car. Maybe she'd misread him. He hadn't been silently hoping she'd stay. She'd seen only what she wanted to see. It had been wishful thinking.

THE LATE-AFTERNOON SUN penetrated the driver's tinted window and beat down on Kate's arm. Wrong time to be headed toward the Sugarloaf. Not only was the sun blazing hot but it had sunk low enough that even with sunglasses on and the visor pulled down she had to squint to see the road in front of her.

She'd turned the air conditioner up full blast and was about to crank up the volume of the CD player to compensate when she saw a massive cloud of dust.

She slowed the car and watched the dust travel the overgrown road toward the old Barker place, which stood in the middle of nowhere and had been deserted three years ago. Quickly she turned off the CD player and the air conditioner. The whir of a motor came from the direction of the traveling dust cloud. Odd. Who would be going down that road? They had to be in a Jeep or ATV or dirt bike, something off-road. Maybe they were joyriding kids. She hoped not. It wasn't safe, not with the barbed wire fencing that had fallen and was strewn about the property. She knew because the Barkers had asked Clint and Joe to keep an eye on the place after two high school kids had gotten hurt during an unauthorized party.

Curious, she pulled onto the shoulder and waited to

see if she could catch a glimpse of the vehicle as it made the turn. The sun was to the left and for a few seconds she got a clear view of the red ATV. The same color as the one Brad had been riding earlier. Of course there were probably a couple dozen red ones in the area, two on the Sugarloaf alone, so it didn't mean that was Brad at the wheel. But that knowledge wasn't enough to chase away the uneasy feeling that persisted in her belly, and then grew stronger when she saw a dark blue sedan slow down behind her and turn off the highway toward the Barker place.

She knew that car. It belonged to Levi Dodd, the Realtor, and it was not the kind of vehicle that would easily travel the overgrown dirt road. So was it following the red ATV? Or were the two drivers headed for a predetermined meeting spot?

Realizing how tense she'd become, she exhaled slowly, her thoughts swirling. She couldn't follow them without being discovered. She couldn't even be sure it was Brad and Dodd. Did she dare call Mitch? No, he was busy checking on the sheriff. Besides, what would she tell him? It *might* be Brad meeting Dodd. That alone told her nothing. For all she knew the Barkers had decided to sell and Brad was interested in buying their old place.

Then, too, Mr. Dodd could easily have spotted her car, so if there was something nefarious going on, they would be cautious, maybe even have backed off by now.

Frustrated, she rubbed her temple, trying to organize her thoughts and contemplating her best course of action. How could Brad be linked to both the sheriff and Levi Dodd? Mitch was investigating the sheriff, and if there was anything on Brad, he'd likely uncover that, too. The Realtor was the new puzzle piece. That's where she could help. But she needed her computer.

She glanced toward the Barker's where most of the dust had settled, and then checked the rearview mirror before pulling onto the highway. Was Levi Dodd from Houston or Dallas? She couldn't remember, but she'd find out. Either way, how did he end up out here trying to drum up business? People tended to hang on to their land come hell or high water. Until the rustlers showed up.

Her heart thudded. Holy crap. Was that what this was about? Her pulse and mind racing, she pressed her foot to the accelerator, anxious to get to her laptop. She had a feeling Levi Dodd just might be the key to this whole mess.

MITCH RUBBED HIS EYES, checked the monitor and then stared out the window into the darkness. The curtains should've been drawn an hour ago, but he hadn't been paying attention. He missed Kate. It was weird not having her here to share what information he'd found, or more appropriately, the lack of information.

He'd come up empty. So had his contact at the FBI, a woman who'd owed him a favor. They'd tracked Sheriff Harding back to the day he graduated from high school. He'd worked for only one other county in his career, his boss there gave him glowing reports and had been sorry to lose him. The only reason he'd left, Mitch was told, was because Harding's wife had been sick and he wanted to move her closer to her family in Houston. The guy was nothing short of a Boy Scout. At least on paper. A sick wife could mean he was financially strapped and vulnerable to thieves willing to supply him with cash. But there was no paper trail to prove it.

Unfortunately, Brad's background was thin. He seemed to be a loner who'd lived in Texas most of his life, hopping from one job to the next. But his record was clean, and there was nothing in his history to warrant suspicion. Still, Mitch was uneasy. And not just because he hadn't liked Brad sniffing around Kate, although he had to work on isolating his personal feelings. The fact remained that it made no sense for the two men to be meeting out in the middle of nowhere.

Mitch's gaze went to his cell phone. It sat on the table next to the monitor so if it had rung he couldn't have missed a call. He picked it up anyway, and checked to make sure Kate hadn't left a message. No surprise that she hadn't, but the confirmation depressed him. Damn, he was tempted to call her, even though he'd sworn to himself that he'd let her have her space.

It was completely his fault that she'd returned to the Sugarloaf. He'd been an ass about ordering her to stay away from Brad, and then topped it off by implying that the guy's only interest in her was in using her. Whether the man was involved in a rustling racket or not, there was plenty of reason he'd want to keep company with a beautiful woman like Kate. But she was still bruised from Dennis's betrayal, and the last thing she needed was another reason to feel like crap.

As much as Mitch wanted to kick himself until next Sunday for his thoughtlessness, he was more worried that her withdrawal might have something to do with him wanting to return and work his family's ranch. Did she think that him being back for good would smother

her? That he expected her to give up her career, her dreams? No matter what happened, he'd always want what was best for Kate. He wanted her happy.

But the truth was, he also wanted her at his side. Hell, one evening away from her told him all he needed to know. He felt lost without her. As if a piece of him was missing. The feeling totally sucked. He'd always been a loner, and never experienced anything like it before.

The knock at the door startled him. His gaze flew to the monitors, and seeing everything was okay, he got up to peer out the window toward the driveway. No car. Yet someone was obviously here, and he clearly hadn't been paying attention or he would've seen their approach. Great.

He hurried down the stairs and opened the front door. "Kate."

"I've found something." She moved past him, carrying a laptop.

He was so damn glad to see her that her words barely registered. "I have an apology to make."

"I think I know who's behind the rustling." She went straight for the stairs. "Let's stick close to the monitors."

He followed her up, glanced at the monitors as he closed the curtains, and then sat next to her on the edge of the bed. She'd opened her laptop and started typing.

"Give me something," he said impatiently.

"It's not about the rustling. That's merely a means to an end. It's about the land." Her gaze stayed on the screen. "Dodd is buying up the abandoned ranches for a company called West End Minerals. At least he's their buying agent."

"Are the sheriff and Brad involved?"

"I don't know. They could be working for Dodd,

setting up vulnerable ranches, striking to drive the owners off. I only know that West End has bought everything in the area, and they've been making a killing on coal and copper lately." She stopped typing, her face flushed with excitement. "Look."

She displayed a commodities exchange chart supporting what she'd said, then switched to a screen showing a county listing of land titles. West End Minerals had been doing a lot of real estate purchasing, all right. She minimized the screen and brought up a map shaded with mineral-rich areas to the north and west.

Mitch shrugged, trying to make sense of this. "We're too far south for coal and too far northeast for copper."

"There was a moderate find here," she said, pointing to the map. "I think they're speculating. The sheriff said there had been reports of the rustlers moving north." She gestured to the map that showed a dense concentration of coal. "Make sense?"

"Yeah. If he's involved, he could've been lying to throw me off, or they're running the same game on the folks up there," Mitch said, his mind racing ahead. And then something occurred to him. "How did you know to look in this direction?"

"I saw Dodd meet with Brad. At least I'm pretty sure they did. I saw them both head toward the Barker's old place."

"Godamn it, Kate, you could've—"

"Don't you dare." She glared angrily at him. In fact, he didn't recall ever seeing her this livid.

"You're right." He took a deep breath. "I'm sorry," he said, even though he thought she was being too touchy. This wasn't about playing the big brother role.

Naturally he'd worry that something might happen to her if... "What?"

She was anxiously looking past him. "Someone's out there."

He spun toward the monitor. It was hard to see with the figures sticking so close to the shadows, but there were two men near the cattle. "Call Joe," Mitch said, grabbing the rifle he kept leaning against the wall at the ready. "Ask him to bring some men from the Sugarloaf."

She surprised him by darting out of the room, and he hoped that she'd heard him. He was halfway down the stairs when he realized she was behind him, and he glanced over his shoulder. She was carrying a rifle.

"What the hell are you doing?" He stopped, and blocked her way. "You aren't going out there."

"The hell I'm not." She tried to push past him. "I'm a damn good shot and you need me."

"I need you to be safe." He gripped her arm. "Please."

With pleading eyes, she said softly, "And I need this."

He swallowed hard. Now she had to assert her independence? "Okay, we're wasting time."

They took Mitch's rental car because it was dark colored, new and quiet. He lowered the windows to listen and left the headlights off out of necessity, making it tough to navigate. While he drove the half mile out to the pens, Kate called Joe for backup, and warned him not to involve the sheriff.

The tense silence in the car was disturbed by the low of disgruntled cattle. As they got closer, Mitch saw the large hulking cattle truck being loaded by two men, working quickly, silently. He cut the engine and allowed the rental car to coast to a stop in front of the truck. Right as he motioned to Kate that he was about to get out, he saw that there was one more man standing on the other side of the truck. Three total. Shit.

Damn, he didn't want Kate to get out of the car. If these guys had guns, they weren't going to be picky about who was holding the rifle. Yet he knew that for her, there was more at stake here than her safety. Helplessness overwhelmed him. He had to focus. They could stall for a few minutes, at least until the cattle were loaded, and hope Joe got here quickly.

He stayed put, raised a restraining hand, and Kate nodded.

After about five long minutes, he heard a man call out, "Is that the last one?"

Another man answered in the affirmative, and Mitch knew this was it. No more stalling. He signaled to Kate, and they both quietly opened their doors. Sweat had broken out at the back of his neck. He couldn't look at Kate holding the rifle. She was right. She was a damn good shot. He had to let it go, or he'd end up being the one who got her killed.

He signaled again, letting her know that they should flank the truck from behind and work their way toward the back. He wanted to get to the men first. If they were armed, logically only one of them would be holding a gun at the ready. That was the man he wanted before Kate showed herself.

As soon as he got within sight of the rustlers, he heard Kate say, "Drop it."

The barrel-chested man holding the gun turned in surprise. He lifted his revolver, and Mitch rushed forward and kicked it out of his hand. Kate turned her rifle on the taller man, who'd stepped out of the shadows.

"Stop where you are, Brad. Put your hands up. I won't hesitate to use this," Kate warned, her voice as steady as the rifle she'd raised to her shoulder.

The third rustler ran. The barrel-chested man dived for his gun. Mitch spun around and with one well-placed karate thrust to the man's gut, sent him flying backward. He was out cold.

"What about the other guy?" Kate asked, keeping her sight on Brad.

Mitch picked up the revolver and stuck it into the waistband of his jeans. "He won't get far."

"Damn." Brad joined his hands behind his neck and shook his head.

Behind them, they could hear reinforcements coming down the dirt road. Neither Mitch or Kate turned to look, but kept their rifles trained on the two men.

Joe and three of the Sugarloaf cowhands rushed to the scene. With them was the sheriff and a deputy.

Mitch cursed violently and swung his rifle toward Harding. "What the hell, Joe?"

"Mitch!" Joe shoved the rifle barrel aside. "It's not what you think. Kate, you, too, put your rifle down."

Ignoring them, Sheriff Harding walked toward Brad. "You get enough?"

Brad cautiously lowered his hands. "To implicate Dodd, but that's all. I think he'll talk, though."

Kate reluctantly lowered the rifle and looked at her brother. "What's going on?"

"We got another one out in the wind," Brad said, indicating the man who'd run off with a jerk of his thumb.

"I doubt he knows anything but someone's gotta pick him up." Brad sighed wearily, and turned to Kate. "Texas Ranger Jake Malone, ma'am," he said with a cocky Brad-like wink. "At your service."

IT WAS NEARLY DAWN by the time Mitch and Kate were alone again. She'd made coffee for Joe and the Sugarloaf cowhands. The sheriff, deputy, Jake and the two other Texas rangers that had been called in to assist hadn't stayed. They'd taken the pair of rustlers into custody and had other arrests to make, starting with Levi Dodd. Besides, the sheriff was still ticked off at Mitch for interfering and forcing them to prematurely step up their plans.

Harding and Jake had suspected Dodd for a while, but they were hoping that by Jake infiltrating the rustling ring they could dig deep enough to incriminate the West End executives who'd hired Dodd to acquire land by any means.

Mitch brought the last two dirty mugs to the kitchen. "Man, Harding was pissed. He looked as if he wanted to shoot me. Jake said that as soon as they saw the plane they knew it was me."

"Well, that was stupid because he could've just said something." Kate dropped the mugs into the sudsy water, nervous now that they were alone again. She had something to say to him that he might not want to hear, but too bad.

"There you go again." Mitch's voice was close to her ear.

She spun around just as he was going to slide his arms around her. He did anyway. "Hey, my hands are wet," she said and looped her arms around his neck, smiling when he made a face. "What did you mean, there I go again?"

"Yes, your hands are very wet." He kissed the tip of her nose. "You were defending me."

"Was I?" She stopped to consider him. "And that's a problem?"

"No, people who love each other do things like that."

Her heart thudded. He'd used the *L* word. "Yes," she said slowly, her legs weak. "I suppose they do."

"That means I will also want to defend and protect you."

Oh, she hoped he didn't suddenly let her go, because she'd sink right to the floor.

"But that doesn't mean I'm trying to be your big brother."

She laughed, feeling her cheeks heat up. "I hope not."

His face got very serious. "The hardest thing I've ever done in my life was let you walk out the door with that rifle." He studied her face. "Do you understand?"

She nodded, a lump rising in her throat. "Thank you."

"I want you safe. I want you happy." He paused. "I want to come back for good. But not if it will upset your life."

She had to clear her throat, afraid she'd be unable to speak. "I want you happy, too, but you won't be happy here." His lips parted in protest; she shook her head. "I'd be lying if I didn't admit I've fantasized about you coming back, but I saw how you looked yesterday while we were flying. I heard the excitement in your voice when you described the places you'd been…."

"I'm not saying I'm never going to leave here or fly again." His eyes bored into hers. "This isn't a spur-of-the-moment decision. I've been thinking about this for a while. It feels right to be here. *You* feel right."

"And if you start missing your old life—"

"There will be aspects I'll miss," he admitted. "But not being with you…" Fear filled his eyes, genuine, honest-to-goodness fear. "I can't even go there."

She hugged his neck so tightly she thought she might hurt him. "Until last night I didn't think you could ever see me as an equal. You proved me wrong."

"Glad I passed muster. I just hope there aren't any more tests in the near future. My heart can't take it."

Kate grinned. "I hope it can take this. I love you, Mitch. This isn't a schoolgirl crush talking. I *love* you."

His eyes briefly closed and his mouth curved in a smile. "I love you, too, Kate Manning, even though your brothers will probably kick my ass all the way back to Florida."

She laughed. "Then we'll fly back together," she said and kissed him.

Epilogue

KATE HUNG THE LAST SHINY red ornament on the Christmas tree and then stood back to survey her work. The messy hodgepodge of old-fashioned glass balls and tiny homemade rag dolls made her smile. But she'd managed to include every Colter keepsake that had graced the family trees for three generations. Only the lopsided muslin angel on the top was missing. As soon as Mitch came back inside with the garland, she'd let him do the honors since he wouldn't need a step stool.

She was anxious for his parents and his sister, Susie, and her kids to arrive tomorrow. She couldn't wait to see the look on their faces when they saw how much Mitch had done with the ranch. He'd worked tirelessly from daybreak to sundown since July to whip the place into shape. Kate had worked alongside him when she could, but mostly she stuck to fixing up the house. Occasionally she missed teaching, although she really enjoyed working as a volunteer tutor at the library in Willowville.

The front door opened and she turned to watch Mitch stomp his boots on the outside rug before coming over the threshold. "We've got company," he said, with a jerk of his head.

"Who?" She hurried to relieve him of some of the garland piled high in his arms.

"Jake Malone. He just pulled up." Mitch unloaded the garland near the banister. "I told him to come on in."

"I hope he finally caught the rest of the people involved in the land grab." They hadn't seen the Texas Ranger for about three months, not since testifying against the rustlers.

"Couldn't ask for a better Christmas present."

"Hey." She elbowed him in the ribs. "The wedding isn't for another two weeks. I'd watch it if I were you."

Mitch grinned, slid an arm around her shoulders and gave her a quick kiss. "You wouldn't change your mind and break my heart, would you?"

"Well, so much for that." Jake stood at the door, a wry look on his face as he lifted his hat off and held it against his chest.

Kate gestured for him to come in. "So much for what."

"I came to ask you out to dinner, but I see Colter finally wised up." Jake shook his head. "I figured there was something going on, you sly devils."

Heat filled Kate's cheeks, and she slid a look at Mitch. The possessive gleam in his eyes thrilled her all the way down to her toes. "I had to practically hit him over the head to knock some sense into him. Can I offer you something to drink?"

"No, thanks, I'm good." Jake glanced at the tree. "I keep forgetting Christmas is only a week away."

"What are you doing for the holiday?" Kate asked.

He shrugged. "Working, probably."

"You could come over. Mitch's family will be here and my brothers and a lot of the hands—"

Jake shook his head. "I usually work."

"If you change your mind, Malone, you're welcome here." Mitch touched the small of Kate's back. "We're getting married the week after, and having a party at the Sugarloaf. The invitation is open then, too."

"Good for you." Jake smiled and moved forward to lightly kiss Kate's cheek. "Really, y'all make a nice couple. I'm happy for you. Maybe I'll have some good news for your wedding day."

Mitch straightened. "You got someone to give up Wellsley?"

"Not yet, but I've got a good lead."

Excited, Kate squeezed Mitch's arm. If it could be proved that the president and CEO of the mineral company had been pulling the strings, all the victims could be compensated.

She and Mitch were all right in the money department, but so many of their neighbors had lost more than they could afford.

"I'll let you know what happens." Jake set his hat back on his head. "I'm going to talk to Sheriff Harding now. He'll keep you informed, but for now this stays between us."

"Absolutely." Mitch shook his hand. "Thanks for everything."

"No problem. Y'all have a nice Christmas."

They said their goodbyes, and as soon as Jake closed the door behind him, Kate threw her arms around Mitch. "Wouldn't that be great if everyone were reimbursed for their cattle?"

"What a Christmas present that would be." Mitch kissed the tip of her nose. "I like Jake. He doesn't give up."

"Hmm, he's awfully good-looking, too."

"Hey."

Kate grinned. "Not that he comes close to you." She hugged him closer. "In two weeks, I'm going to have the best-looking husband in all of Texas."

His earnest gaze roamed her face. "Why do we have to wait?"

"Because your family wants to be here for the ceremony." Her insides warmed at the raw longing in his eyes. "Two weeks isn't very long."

"It is when I've already waited a lifetime," he whispered, and kissed her slow and deep until she swore her feet had left the ground.

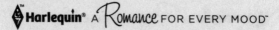

Harlequin® A *Romance* FOR EVERY MOOD™

HEART & HOME

Heartwarming romances where love can
happen right when you least expect it.

Harlequin® American Romance®
Lively stories about homes, families
and communities like the ones you know.
This is romance the all-American way!

Silhouette® Special Edition
A woman in her world—living and loving.
Celebrating the magic of creating a family
and developing romantic relationships.

Harlequin® Superromance®
Unexpected, exciting and emotional
stories about life and falling in love.

Look for these and many other Harlequin and Silhouette
romance books wherever books are sold, including most
bookstores, supermarkets, drugstores and discount stores.

REQUEST YOUR FREE BOOKS!

2 FREE NOVELS
FROM THE ROMANCE COLLECTION
PLUS 2 FREE GIFTS!

YES! Please send me 2 FREE novels from the Romance Collection and my 2 FREE gifts (gifts are worth about $10). After receiving them, if I don't wish to receive any more books, I can return the shipping statement marked "cancel." If I don't cancel, I will receive 4 brand-new novels every month and be billed just $5.74 per book in the U.S. or $6.24 per book in Canada. That's a saving of at least 28% off the cover price. It's quite a bargain! Shipping and handling is just 50¢ per book in the U.S. and 75¢ per book in Canada.* I understand that accepting the 2 free books and gifts places me under no obligation to buy anything. I can always return a shipment and cancel at any time. Even if I never buy another book, the two free books and gifts are mine to keep forever.

194/394 MDN FDC5

Name   (PLEASE PRINT)

Address   Apt. #

City   State/Prov.   Zip/Postal Code

Signature (if under 18, a parent or guardian must sign)

Mail to the **Reader Service:**
IN U.S.A.: P.O. Box 1867, Buffalo, NY 14240-1867
IN CANADA: P.O. Box 609, Fort Erie, Ontario L2A 5X3

Not valid for current subscribers to the Romance Collection
or the Romance/Suspense Collection.

Want to try two free books from another line?
Call 1-800-873-8635 or visit www.ReaderService.com.

* Terms and prices subject to change without notice. Prices do not include applicable taxes. Sales tax applicable in N.Y. Canadian residents will be charged applicable taxes. Offer not valid in Quebec. This offer is limited to one order per household. All orders subject to credit approval. Credit or debit balances in a customer's account(s) may be offset by any other outstanding balance owed by or to the customer. Please allow 4 to 6 weeks for delivery. Offer available while quantities last.

Your Privacy—The Reader Service is committed to protecting your privacy. Our Privacy Policy is available online at www.ReaderService.com or upon request from the Reader Service.

We make a portion of our mailing list available to reputable third parties that offer products we believe may interest you. If you prefer that we not exchange your name with third parties, or if you wish to clarify or modify your communication preferences, please visit us at www.ReaderService.com/consumerschoice or write to us at Reader Service Preference Service, P.O. Box 9062, Buffalo, NY 14269. Include your complete name and address.

Harlequin *Desire*

ALWAYS POWERFUL, PASSIONATE AND PROVOCATIVE.

NEW YORK TIMES AND USA TODAY
BESTSELLING AUTHOR

BRENDA JACKSON

PRESENTS A BRAND-NEW TALE
OF SEDUCTION

TEMPTATION

Millionaire security expert and rancher Zeke Travers always separates emotion from work. Until a case leads him to Sheila Hopkins—and the immediate, scorching heat between them. Suddenly, Zeke is tempted to break the rules. And it's only a matter of time before he gives in....

**Available November
wherever books are sold.**

www.Harlequin.com

SDBJ1111IBC

ISBN-13:978-0-373-36552-4

36552

0 65373 36552 0

red-hot reads

Blaze

From crush...to a full-on collision!

Kate Manning's "blast from the past" has blown back to her quiet west Texas town! Mitch Colter was once the sum of all Kate's fantasies. But he was a few years older and her brothers' best friend, and her fantasies stayed exactly that. Now however, Kate's got seduction in mind and a point to prove: she won't miss out on Mitch a second time.

Mitch can't believe the woman his "little Katie" has become. She's beautiful, has a body that gives him all kinds of naughty ideas and, best of all, she's lost none of her fiery spirit and take-no-prisoners sense of humor. So, when Kate comes a-calling—he can't resist—and won't! But will their luck be better the second time around?

$3.99 U.S.

ISBN-13:978-0-373-36552-4

50399

9 780373 365524

EAN

PASSION

a HARLEQUIN® BLAZE™
book from

HARLEQUIN®
www.Harlequin.com